REDEMPTION

Rob Douglas

SilverWood

Published in 2019 by SilverWood Books

SilverWood Books Ltd
14 Small Street, Bristol, BS1 1DE, United Kingdom
www.silverwoodbooks.co.uk

ISBN 978-1-78132-886-6 (paperback)
ISBN 978-1-78132-887-3 (ebook)

British Library Cataloguing in Publication Data
A CIP catalogue record for this book is available from
the British Library

Page design and typesetting by SilverWood Books
Printed on responsibly sourced paper

To my family

Chapter 1

Bob Kenton removed his glove and wiped the back of his hand across his brow. He stared at the black-streaked sweat. He had been on duty for thirty of the last thirty-six hours and was exhausted. Despite his best efforts and those of his firefighting team, the blaze burning through the woodland refused to be brought under control. They had succeeded in slowing the spread but they could not halt it.

This was the fifth year that he had led his team battling fires in his patch of northern California. Five years running, he thought. It's like a vendetta. Each year the fires were fiercer and each year the state lost more homes and more lives. He watched the flames, transfixed. "This is getting personal!" he muttered as he put his glove back on and headed out to the fire.

On the other side of the Pacific, Niko Manumoto stood in a clearing some 300 feet above her home town. Niko often walked up the hill – she liked the fresh air, and the exercise did her good. She felt the ground tremble slightly beneath her. It wasn't too alarming; tremors were felt often here and they rarely caused a problem. She frowned as she saw a dust cloud rise above the town, but she couldn't spot any specific damage. Suddenly the sound of tsunami sirens filled the air. She looked out to sea and watched as a white line on the ocean grew increasingly larger as it approached the town. Already, she could see people running and heading for the hills on either side. She stood rooted to the spot as the white line became a huge wave that slammed into the small fishing town at the head of its narrow inlet, an inlet that channelled the wave, making it even higher. As Niko looked on, the tsunami momentarily seemed to consume the town and its fleeing residents. A handful of people had reached high enough ground but from where Niko was standing all she could see was churning, swirling water. Suddenly, the wave retreated, leaving total destruction in its wake. Niko's home town had changed beyond all recognition.

Further south, in New Plymouth on New Zealand's North Island, Rob and Aroha Blennan were gazing up at Mount Taranaki. For the first time in living memory, plumes of smoke were rising from the crater. They had started about a week ago. Today there were tremors in the ground. The government had started issuing warnings and advising non-essential workers to move out of the area.

"What the hell is going on?" asked Rob. "The mountain has been quiet for almost two hundred years."

"I spoke to my grandmother today," said Aroha. "She said that mountain was angry."

"Really?" said Rob. "I know you locals treat the mountain as a living being, but I guess this is just geological. I doubt a mountain can be angry."

"My grandmother would disagree with you," said Aroha seriously, as she got into the car.

They drove away, heading north to stay with Rob's brother who lived further up the coast.

Chapter 2

Some 8.6 light years away, on the planet Qrxa, the fourth planet in the Sirius star system, Landro and Vendra were waiting in the anteroom to Chairman Vrin's office. Landro was tall, just over seven feet, dark-skinned, and had long silver hair which he wore tied back. Vendra was only slightly shorter, similarly dark-skinned and also had silver hair. Both wore shaped dark-blue tunics over trousers, and a belt with various devices attached.

"This isn't the first time we've been here," said Landro, "although I am not sure what it is about this time."

"I know the council had a long meeting yesterday about an S211-class planet that is causing concern – maybe that's it. It won't be the first time that we have been asked to go on a reconnaissance mission and find out what's happening on the ground," replied Vendra.

Landro nodded. He had for many years been an envoy the council would send to help deal with difficult and challenging situations in the galaxy. Vendra usually accompanied him. She was a Technology and Operations officer who had spent time on military missions in the past but recently had joined Landro on his diplomatic missions.

The door to the anteroom opened and a small figure appeared. Under five feet, and slim, he had a large head and slanting teardrop-shaped eyes. He looked at Landro and Vendra and gave a small wave.

"Good to see you, Tzok," said Landro. "Do you know what this is about?"

"No," said Tzok.

Landro waited but Tzok said nothing more. Landro wasn't surprised. The Sirians tended to say no more than was necessary. But Tzok's presence suggested that the meeting might be serious. Tzok was a highly-experienced senior officer.

The lights next to the chairman's office changed colour, the door opened and the message came over their neural networks to enter.

Chairman Vrin was seated at a desk at the far end of the room. He greeted them in a similar manner – a small wave – and motioned for them to take a seat from the chairs set out in front of him: two large seats and a smaller one. Vrin was also a Sirian.

"As you know," said Vrin, "the Grand Council oversees all worlds within the known galaxy. It focuses particularly on worlds which, for one reason or another, are problematic. Worlds on the edge of developing interplanetary travel or subspace are all vetted in case the arrival of their inhabitants causes disruption or even chaos. All and any sanctions can be taken against a world deemed unsuitable for expansion."

Landro tried, unsuccessfully, to catch Vendra's eye. This was Vrin's standard introduction to any mission, and he had heard it several times before.

Vrin continued. "Usually worlds are coached and channelled into constructive development rather than set back.

But their inhabitants have to be willing to be guided and to be able to demonstrate that they have the capacity to learn and develop. They must never be a threat to the stability of the known universe.

"We have been observing S211-376 for centuries. Ever since the interference of the Wei, millennia ago, the equilibrium of this world has been destroyed. Their genetic meddling has left one predominant species that now dominates completely. Although the convulsions which accompanied the departure of the Wei resulted in a technological decline, and despite endless warfare among the inhabitants, not just against other species on the planet but against each other, they have begun to recover some technological momentum. In this they – or at least elements, mainly military – are receiving help from other races.

"Your task is to judge whether there is any chance for these inhabitants to be constructive and peaceful members of the galactic community, or whether we need to undo the genetic engineering and allow the world and its other species to recover from its despoliation and abuse in the hope that evolution will allow another sentient, and less warlike, species to develop.

"There is an urgency here as other races are in contact and encouraging division between the nations of the planet and among its inhabitants. These contacts are limited to small groups of mainly military forces of one nation. It is also clear that the patience of the planet itself has run out and it is creating natural disasters on a scale that is threatening all life on the planet.

"You will make open contact and engage in a dialogue with the people of the planet before you decide how to proceed. All the information you need is loaded on your ship. You will depart as soon as possible."

Landro, Vendra and Tzok were dismissed and left the office.

"What do we know about S211-376?" asked Landro.

"We'll find out when we get to whatever vessel is taking us there. It'll all be on the computer. I am sure you will have plenty of time to get up to speed," said Vendra, laughing.

They agreed a time to meet at the space elevator and went their separate ways to prepare for the journey.

Chapter 3

Twelve hours later they arrived at the docking port to meet the shuttle that would take them to their ship. The space elevator had taken them to the off-world complex that lay above the planet. There were several such off-world complexes – some were primarily residential but this one was mainly a space port with construction and maintenance facilities. Several vessels were moored directly to the complex, but larger vessels floated further out and they needed to take a shuttle.

Landro gave a low whistle as they boarded their ship. "This is some vessel," he said, in awe. "I have never been on one of these."

The ship was a research ship, one of only three such vessels. She was huge. Including all probes she measured more than 2.5 miles in length. The drive area alone was one mile long. Landro turned to Tzok: "Why is she so enormous?"

Tzok replied. "The length of the drive area is required to generate the zero-point fields that allow the ship to fold into and pass through subspace. There is a propulsion system for normal space travel and an anti-gravity system that allows the ship to get close to a particular world."

"And what equipment does she carry? She looks as if she has a lot," asked Vendra.

"The ship does carry a lot. There is equipment here that can terraform worlds or reconfigure them. There is other equipment that allows the ship to monitor and influence the energy flows of the worlds and their inhabitants that it encounters.. And there is observation and interpretation equipment."

"Are there any weapon systems?" asked Landro, "in case the going gets tough."

"Well, it is not a warship; it is primarily a research and exploration vessel. However, in the unlikely event that we have to defend ourselves I am confident its array of equipment will make it virtually impregnable."

"I hope you're right," said Landro with a slight grimace.

The shuttle docked and the group disembarked. Two Sirians met them, showed them their quarters and led them to the bridge and the control room.

"What is the name of this ship?" Landro asked Tzok.

"*Research Vessel 2*," replied Tzok.

"That's very dull!" said Landro. "We need something more evocative. How about *Touching the Heavens*?"

Tzok looked at him quizzically and said nothing.

Vendra raised her eyebrows slightly. "*RV2* seems fine but I know you like something more exciting so let's go with your idea."

Landro checked the readings on the screen. He knew this was superfluous since the ship's computer was far more competent than he was at identifying any problems and fixing them, but psychologically he felt reassured to be doing it.

"Tell us about S211-376," he instructed the computer.

The computer provided a more detailed description of the planet. Then it announced in its strangely disembodied voice: "This is the planet from which your ancestors, Landro and Vendra, were taken some 20,000 years ago."

Landro and Vendra looked at each other, shocked. They knew the stories of their arrival in the Sirius system but had not known the Sirian designation of the planet. They now realised that they were probably being sent there because they were both products of that same genetic engineering. Their ancestors had been taken off the planet before the Wei left. For reasons that were never totally clear, the Wei had removed a large number of their ancestors from the planet and after various journeys, the group had ended up at Qrxa where they had been accepted, albeit with some reluctance by the native Sirians.

"Why didn't Chairman Vrin mention this?" said Landro.

"Why would he?" answered Tzok. "It shouldn't make any difference to you. A Sirian does not tackle a mission differently because he or she goes to a planet where there are other Sirians."

"That," said Vendra, "is a very Sirian response. But I think it will be strange to engage with other humans on a planet where there has been no open contact for what will be well over 20,000 of the planet's years."

Touching the Heavens disconnected its tethers and headed away from Qrxa.

Chapter 4

Landro still found the speed of subspace travel astonishing. It seemed almost instantaneous – one moment they had been moving away from their base on Qrxa and then, within a couple of days, they had arrived, out between the fifth and sixth planets of their S211 system.

Vendra and Landro looked at the sensors and long-range cameras. This particular solar system – S211-376 (the 376 differentiated it from other S211 systems) – had comprised one heavily-inhabited planet. Technologically, the inhabitants had achieved limited off-world capability. There were three manned space stations in low-earth orbit, many communication and Earth observation satellites, and various probes fanning out across the system.

Landro hoped that none of the planet's probes would have picked up their arrival. Even though they had been visible for only a split second, the interference to the space around them as they came out of subspace was measurable and observable.

Vendra turned and said, "We are already picking up more information than our earlier probes discovered. There is confirmation of a settlement on the moon of P3, the main inhabited planet, possibly by another species, maybe a remnant of the Wei. We seem to have underground cities on P4, although we cannot trace any inhabitants."

Landro said, "Let's prepare for our visit." With that, he asked the ship to move closer to P3. Despite the cloaking, he knew that the movement of such a large vessel could create perturbations, and he did not want to be detected. Once they were close enough, they increased the surveillance and he and Vendra connected themselves to the computers to review the data being received. This included downloads from earlier probes that had been sent through and which had been monitoring the radio and TV stations for many decades. The computer sifted and produced a summary of the major events over those decades, and gave political, geographical and environmental overviews.

P3, with its 6 billion-plus inhabitants, was overcrowded and polluted, fragmented into squabbling nation states of various sizes and various political beliefs. Strong strands of religious beliefs compounded this as prejudices and intolerances were deeply embedded in people's minds. Both Landro and Vendra could see why the council was so concerned. Certain nations were forging ahead at increasing rates of technological advancement and yet much of P3's population remained unaffected by this technology, struggling with even the most basic necessities to stay alive. As for other species, virtually all other land-based species had been subordinated to the main population – either tamed, destroyed or kept in special reserves. The more advanced seafaring species had more scope for freedom but even they found their food sources dwindling and themselves hunted, often just for sport.

The environment was polluted, and the natural resources below the surface ruthlessly exploited.

Data gleaned by the ship's computers showed that there was an awareness in some parts of the world of the appalling damage being inflicted and its unsustainability. However, disappointingly, there was no sign of any meaningful change of direction.

This world was living on a knife-edge – its atmosphere polluted and its climate changing as a result of that and natural cycles. Moreover, the very planet's own awareness and consciousness – known locally as Gaia – had called for help and was taking matters into its own hands, as Vrin had indicated.

As well as absorbing the data, Landro and Vendra used their implants to learn the main languages of the planet. There were thousands of such languages, some spoken only by handfuls of people but there were others spoken by millions, and in some case billions.

They had no trouble mastering the pronunciation as their vocal chords matched those of the inhabitants.

"I wonder which of these is closest to the language our ancestors spoke," wondered Landro out loud.

"Your language died out," replied the computer, to his surprise, "although some old texts of later versions have been found. They tell the story of your ancestors, but hardly anyone on the planet treats them as anything other than myths and legends."

What was clear was that the inhabitants of P3 were unaware of their history. They saw their development as totally linear – they were more advanced than their predecessors, and the intervention of the Wei was treated as fanciful stories of primitive tribespeople. The idea that P3 may have had more advanced technologies that had been lost in the civil wars of the Wei, and the subsequent natural disasters was dismissed, if discussed at all.

"It's odd that the inhabitants have no single name for their planet," observed Vendra. "Every language uses a different name."

They continued their observations and research for six weeks. Then they were ready to progress to the next stage.

Chapter 5

At RAF Fylingdales, Jim Bayliss had just come on duty and was watching his screen. He grabbed a coffee on what had seemed like another quiet, normal day tracking satellites and planes, all of which had identity markers on them. Right now though, he was perplexed. On the screen was a shadow which seemed to appear and disappear. At first, he thought that it was a screen malfunction as it was so faint, but the way the shadow moved before disappearing made him wonder. He called over to the group captain, Sarah Dale.

"Group Captain, Ma'am, sorry to bother you but would you have a look at my screen, please?"

Sarah came over to his desk. "Are you sure it's not a computer malfunction? It is so indistinct and is bigger than any plane or space vehicle we know of."

However, after fifteen minutes, Sarah was concerned enough to ring Space HQ at High Wycombe. Group Captain Roger Merrit took the call. She connected him to their screens. He was equally puzzled and, like Sarah, felt that it could not be ignored. They ran more tests on the recording, but the shadowy images remained.

Roger said, "Let me talk to the MOD."

At the MOD, Air Vice Marshall John Penton was briefed on Roger and Sarah's concerns via a conference call. Having checked that they had cross-verified their data and that it really wasn't a malfunction, he said, "Okay, Roger, you talk to the Americans, but keep it low profile. Sarah, can you call ESA and ask them if the International Space Station is picking up anything? No need to bother the minister yet."

Two hundred miles above the Earth, *Touching the Heavens* had halted its descent. Landro and Vendra had headed down to the middle section and boarded a smaller craft. It was a substantial craft in its own right. Apart from state-of-the-art sensors and bio-computing capabilities, it also had a substantial defensive capability. Even if their ancestors had come from here, this was still an alien planet, and alien planets were not always too welcoming. Although they were confident about their abilities to resist any known technologies on the planet, they didn't want any surprises. The only thing that the shuttle lacked was the subspace capabilities.

Following their immersion in Earth's history, they had renamed the craft *Sumer*. It moved away from *Touching the Heavens*, paused to confirm all systems were working and then headed earthwards. It was the turbulence of that departure that Fylingdales had picked up.

At 100,000 feet, *Sumer* uncloaked, and Landro sent their first message.

"Air traffic control, this is the research vessel *Sumer*. We are descending through London airspace and will halt above Hyde Park at a height of 600 feet."

An astonished voice replied, "Who the hell are you?

Where are you? Do not, I repeat, do not enter London airspace – you have no authority."

"Air traffic control, I repeat, we are the research vessel *Sumer* from the Sirius star system. We are not asking permission – we are informing you of our arrival so that you can divert other traffic. We do not want any accidents as we enter your airspace."

John Penton was with the chief of the defence staff and the minister, whom he had decided to brief, updating them on the latest developments, when one of his staff rushed in.

"Air traffic control has reported that a plane without a transponder has announced their descent on London. They have it on their radar – it appears to be oval and around 1,000 feet in diameter. They say it doesn't look like a fake."

"My God!" said the minister. "What do we do?"

"Scramble a couple of squadrons for starters," replied the chief of the defence staff. "Did ATC have any more information?"

The man paled. "ATC added that it announced itself in flawless English as the research vessel *Sumer* from the Sirius star system. They said they were heading for Hyde Park."

"Hyde Park!" yelled the minister. "What the hell are they doing going there? And why are they here?"

"Well," said the chief, looking rather quizzically at the minister, "it appears they are heading this way, so we need to find out why. Instruct air traffic control in the meantime to tell them not to land in London but steer them to another base, preferably one of the East Anglian air force bases. Tell the Typhoons to deliver the same message in person. Minister, you and I need to head over to Downing Street, urgently. John, you call the Americans – tell them that we don't think this is a hoax and that we will get back to them as soon as we have clarified what exactly is happening."

Sumer continued its descent. Air traffic control repeatedly ordered them to move away from London, informing them that they had no authority to proceed and that the RAF would be forced to intervene if they continued with their present trajectory.

Landro calmly repeated that he was not asking permission, but that he was advising them so that they could ensure there would be no accidents, and that the RAF should be informed that they were here peacefully but that they would defend themselves if attacked.

Squadron Leader Steve Matthews had taken off from RAF Alconbury in something of a hurry. He had two other planes in flight.

"Is this for real?" asked Pilot Officer Geoff Andrews, "or is this another MOD test?"

"Don't know, Geoff. They're saying it isn't a hoax."

"God, I hope it doesn't end up like *Independence Day*," said Giles, the other PO, over the intercom.

"I am sure it won't," replied the squadron leader as they tore south, although the same thought had already crossed his mind.

"Jesus!" they cried in unison as they saw the huge-diameter saucer gently descending. "That is enormous. And where are its engines? How does it do that?"

"Alien spacecraft, this is Squadron Leader Matthews of the Royal Air Force. You are not authorised to be in this area, and I must insist that you follow me to land at RAF Alconbury."

Landro replied, "Squadron Leader Matthews, this is the research vessel *Sumer*. We have our destination, thank you, and we will proceed there. We wish you no harm. But feel free to escort us. Please ensure that you keep a distance of at least 1,500 feet to avoid any unintended harm from our engines."

Matthews paused. What now? He went back to the group captain at RAF Alconbury. "Should we engage?"

The group captain told him to do nothing as he rang High Wycombe. His own instinct was definitely not to open fire. It would not be a good start for mankind to open fire on the first openly visiting alien spacecraft in the history of the Earth. But what if it wasn't peaceful?

In the meantime, the jets circled around *Sumer.*

"Don't get too close, Giles," warned Steve.

"I'm just having a look," said Giles.

Suddenly his engines cut out as his electronics failed.

"Whoa! I've been hit, I think. I have no power."

At that moment, just as his jet started to plummet and he was about to engage the ejector seat, it stopped mid-air. There was total silence and the Typhoon simply hung in the air.

"I asked you not to get too close. Your systems are not resilient enough. I have your plane in a tractor beam and I will lower it to the ground. Tell your pilot not to eject."

"Roger that," said Giles, as he sat in the deathly silent plane as it was lowered very gently towards the ground. "I hope to God this works."

The plane was set down carefully on the runway at RAF Northolt. A very shaken Giles stepped out to the astonishment of the fire crews and the wing commander.

"Are you okay, Giles?" said Steve, who had watched in disbelief.

"Yes, I am fine, thank you, sir."

"He is fine," said the voice from *Sumer,* "but I am afraid your plane will need new electronics."

At 500 feet, circled by the two remaining jets, *Sumer* came to an almost silent halt above Hyde Park, casting a huge shadow from the midday sun.

Chapter 6

As the spacecraft sat silently above Hyde Park, crowds began to gather in the surrounding areas. The police arrived and attempted to push people back, but they were no match for the crowds. Camera crews arrived and word quickly spread around the world. Reactions varied.

In London there was a tremendous buzz of excitement and little panic. The government had rapidly broadcast the exchanges with air traffic control, which, together with the news about the gentle landing of the Typhoon with the fried electronics, was reassuring.

In Washington, the hotline with Downing Street was in constant use. In the White House, the president, Steve McIerney, met with his senior advisers and military. The first question they all asked was: why would an Extra Terrestrial go to London for its first contact and not the United States? Was it a threat to the United States and their substantial space assets?

The president looked at the head of US Space Command. "How come none of your people picked this thing up? I thought you said that nothing could approach the Earth without us knowing."

"We're trying to understand that right now, Mr President. Our teams are reviewing the data streams from our more distant probes as well as the probes in geostationary orbit. It must have had some sort of cloaking device. Perhaps like our own X-67 but much more sophisticated. And it must have an anti-gravity drive to be able just to hover like that. The Brits have picked up virtually no sound from the craft. We have a team on the way to support the local US Air Force people based in the UK."

"The fact remains that a 1,000-foot-circumference vehicle has landed on the Earth from outer space, and we knew nothing about it. Are there any others out there?"

"We're searching now, Mr President. We're working through Fylingdales as well as our off-earth assets."

"Well, I need you to look harder. And I need you to run some scenarios: if it is peaceful, what is it doing here? If it is hostile, what might it do? What is the significance of it landing in London? What is the significance of it not landing in the US? And one last thing: talk to the guys at Nellis and find out what they think."

In London, Prime Minister Polly Hawkins stood in the garden of 10 Downing Street and looked out towards Hyde Park. She had been prime minster for four years now, but had been an unexpected choice of her party after her predecessor had resigned following a sex scandal. Although admittedly Polly had been a compromise candidate, she came with less baggage than any other candidate. She had established herself quickly, had gone to the country after a year and her party was returned to power with an increased majority. She was popular and her ratings remained high... to the frustration of the opposition parties.

In response to the breaking news, Polly had immediately called a COBRA meeting – the security committee that swung into action in response to a security situation. The PM laughed to herself as she reflected that no one would have envisaged a security crisis such as this.

Her team had wanted her to head off to the safety of the bunkers at High Wycombe, but it seemed to her, looking at the ship, that if it was indeed malevolent, being in High Wycombe wasn't going to make much difference.

She thought for a moment and then said to the team, "If it can transmit to air traffic control, we must be able to transmit back. Get me the channel. I am going to talk to them."

Her National Security Adviser tried to dissuade her but she insisted.

Ten minutes later, accompanied by her staff and military advisers, she stood by the microphone and began to speak. "Research vessel *Sumer*, I am Polly Hawkins, Prime Minister of the United Kingdom of Great Britain and Northern Ireland. If you are here in peace, then welcome to our country and to our planet. I would like to talk to you about your mission here and the reason for your visit."

She paused. Despite the seriousness of this event, she couldn't help feeling amused – she sounded like her sons playing with their Space Lego when they were younger.

Her reverie was cut short by the speaker crackling into life.

"Prime Minister Hawkins, thank you for your welcome," said a voice with a faintly mid-Atlantic accent. I am Commander Landro. I am co-heading the mission to Earth and am in joint command of the research vessel *Sumer*. We would like to meet you too – thank you for your invitation. May I suggest that you come to Hyde Park and we will arrange to transport you aboard our vessel? You will understand our concern at this stage about leaving our ship in case of a hostile response."

"Well, Commander Landro, you will also understand that visiting your ship with no knowledge of why you are here or what your intentions are is equally uncomfortable. There are a lot of very nervous people down here."

After a brief silence, the reply came: "We understand. Let us meet near our ship but on the ground. Our shields can protect us there. I should also state that I want our meeting to be broadcast live…"

The prime minister thought for a moment. Against the advice of ministers and military, she said, "I agree."

Chapter 7

A meeting time of 10.00am had been agreed. The Government issued a message urging everyone to stay calm and the police began to make the area secure. With some nervousness, crews erected a marquee below and to the side of the ship hovering over Hyde Park.

Overnight, conversations had continued around the globe. The feedback from Nellis Air Force Base to the president came back quickly: be very careful of these space travellers. They are unlikely to have the best interests of the United States at heart, nor those of its people, for that matter. The president thought for some time whether he should ring the British PM. If he did, however, he would have to explain whom he had been talking to, and that was not a conversation that he wanted to have right now.

Finally, he made up his mind and rang to wish her luck. His only advice was to warn her against being too optimistic about the reasons for the ship's arrival. He then agreed with the recommendation of his military advisers to increase military preparedness, including an option of targeting Hyde Park with their space-based lasers and the recently developed plasma weapons carried on the X-67B.

Dawn arrived. There had been no movement from the ship and it appeared inert, apart from lights around the perimeter of the vessel and a very low, barely discernible hum. Efforts to scan the hull and find out more information had been unsuccessful.

At 9.45am Prime Minister Polly Hawkins left Downing Street. Accompanying her was the deputy chief of the defence staff, the minister for defence and her private secretary. She had given them all the opportunity not to join her, but everyone had insisted. The deputy PM and the chief of the defence staff had meanwhile gone to the bunkers in High Wycombe. The King had also been advised to remove himself from Buckingham Palace, but had refused.

The press and media had already gathered in the marquee. Far beyond them were the public who had been gathering in their thousands since the night before. Several people were holding up placards with 'The End is Nigh', 'Save us' and 'Save our Planet' and there were even a couple in Klingon. Rooftops were occupied by police and soldiers looking out for any attempts to sabotage the ship.

At 9.55am Polly arrived at the tent. She stepped out of the car and walked to the entrance of the tent, where she waited. She wondered what face she should wear – how do you look when you are about to meet the first alien from another planet, albeit one that seemingly speaks perfect English? How would she react if it had some utterly alien body, with tentacles, or worse, eight legs? She tried to play down the drama. Remember, she said to herself, this is the biggest worldwide audience you will ever have, so don't blow it.

At 10.00 as the chimes of Big Ben began, a small craft emerged from the underside of the ship. It was about twenty feet long and shaped like a teardrop. It slowly…and almost silently…drifted down and landed right in front of the tent.

Apart from the sound of the cameras and the hushed comments of the commentators, there was total silence. Then it seemed as if the side of the craft started to melt. A tall, slim hominid emerged, well over seven feet tall, dressed in a silver tunic with various devices attached to it. It had darkish skin but incongruously silver hair.

The vehicle had landed between the crowds and the tent, but still enough people were able to see the alien. It turned…and waved to the crowd. After a moment, cheers filled the air and people started to wave and holler. The alien waved again and then approached the PM. Polly was around six feet tall but felt dwarfed by the being.

It smiled benignly and said, "I am Commander Landro. You must be Prime Minister Hawkins." The alien offered the prime minister his hand.

His head was large and Polly felt like a child as she took his hand and shook it. She realised she needed to stop staring and say something. Her first reaction was that he seemed to be human and she was about to blurt that out but then remembering herself, said instead, "Welcome. You are our first visitor from another world."

"Thank you for your welcome. Actually, I am not your first visitor. There have been many visits over many centuries but mine is the first in the last 10,000 years to be deliberately so public. And, yes, to answer your unspoken thought, I am human. My ancestors left this planet over 20,000 years ago and there are now human colonies on a number of planets. But there are many other species, many hominid, many not. Shall we go to the tent?"

Landro and the PM moved to the dais at the front of

the tent and stood at two microphones, each with a podium. Landro's towering height was apparent and a technician came nervously forward to adjust the height of the microphone to its maximum. It was still too low. There were chairs but it was clear that they would fail to accommodate Landro. The press and media and various officials were at the front.

Landro began. "I suggest you all ask me questions and I will answer."

Polly felt she should assert herself and briskly interjected. "Well, I will begin and when I have finished, we can open up the floor. To start with, can you please tell us who you are, where you are from and why you are here."

Landro smiled at her then turned to face the audience, still smiling. "My name is Landro of the Dvna and I am joint commander of this research expedition. I have come from what you call the Sirius star system, from a planet called Qrxa, which has many similarities to yours. Most importantly it has a similar atmosphere, which is why I am able to breathe here comfortably enough. I am part of a colony of humans living on that planet, but the main population are Sirians, also hominids but with some different features. The Sirians are an advanced spacefaring species with highly advanced technological skills and scientific knowledge.

"These advanced skills include implants, and it is through such implants that I learnt to speak your language of English. I have also learnt Russian, Spanish and Chinese.

"I was sent here by the council that monitors our galaxy and that contains representatives of many planets and species. The council monitors developing worlds. We have been monitoring your world for some time, particularly since the end of the domination of your world by the Wei some

10,000 Earth years ago. Their genetic experiments here caused much concern, and continue to do so."

He stopped. There was silence.

The PM stared at him and then said, "The Wei? Who are the Wei? We have never heard of them and we are not aware of any genetic experiments here."

Very slowly Leandro looked at her and then at the cameras. "Humans are the product of the genetic experiment…" He paused before continuing, "Yes, you did know about it. You have just chosen to ignore it, remembering it imperfectly and thinking it was myths and legends and not your history.

"The Wei are known in some of your legends as the Annunaki, which is a corruption of the name of the particular group of Wei who came here. They came here 30,000 years ago on a research mission, looking in particular for certain rare minerals. One of these was gold, which they needed mainly for technological reasons, although they also wanted it for trade. They discovered huge deposits of gold in what you call southern Africa.

"The Wei have a particular interest and skill in biology and the manipulation of genes and DNA. Initially, there were not enough of them to do the mining, and the nature of the seams meant that the machines they had with them were inadequate. It was in any case difficult for them to breathe the atmosphere on the planet and so they were largely confined to the two large spaceships that had brought them here.

"They tried to train the most advanced primates to do the work but without success. So they took those primates and started tinkering with their DNA, in particular splicing their own DNA into the primates' DNA to create a hybrid.

35

There were several failures but in the end they created what we would call the modern human. Enough of them were developed to provide the labour in the mines. As well as being created, the humans bred and produced more on their own.

"This continued over several centuries. Meanwhile the Wei, who by then had numbered several hundred, debated whether they wanted to stay here permanently. This led to a major row, with one group wanting to move on and explore...which is in their blood...and the other wanting to adapt their breathing so that they could remain. A small number of the latter group made the changes and came down on to Earth, where they settled. They also interbred with their human creations. This caused a huge rift with the first group and indeed with the rest of the second group. In all their biological experimentation, it had been taboo to the Wei to breed with their creations. The first group decided to leave and discussed whether to destroy the second group and indeed all their human creations, as they would no longer have any use for them. A war followed, and several of the Wei communities on Earth were destroyed with the equivalent of nuclear weapons. One of these was an island city that you know as Atlantis. Its destruction caused huge tidal waves and changed the climate for decades. The original Wei died in the war, as did many of their hybrid offspring and many of the hybridised humans that lived with them in the city.

"Until the second group of Wei had come to Earth, the humans had been bred as labourers and received no training or education beyond what was required to do their mainly manual work. When the Wei interbred, they also started to develop the intellectual side of humans alongside their own hybrid offspring, giving them knowledge of the stars and teaching them the basis of mathematics and technological skills as well as literacy.

"The cataclysm following the brief war destroyed most of that. The few humans that survived were those in more remote areas, and with few exceptions they were the less well educated. A number of the offspring of the Wei/ human couplings also survived and the two groups lived in uneasy coexistence with occasional interrelationships, but there were genetic problems and over time this group gradually disappeared. They were bigger and lived longer than normal humans. They are remembered in your mythology as the giants."

Landro stopped. There was total silence, broken finally by the PM.

"So you are saying that we are the result of a genetic experiment?"

"Precisely."

"And how come you escaped?"

"We didn't escape. Another group of Wei came to the Earth and took us as part of a trade. At that point there was a surplus of humans. We were subsequently traded again in the Sirius system where some of us have remained and others joined expeditions to other systems. Fortunately, the Sirians decided to keep us alive, although they were and remain deeply concerned by the hybridisation that took place."

"Have you come alone? Are there Sirians with you?"

"No, I am not alone and yes, there are Sirians with me."

"Will we meet them?"

"You will meet one of my human companions when we next meet."

"Why did you come to London?"

Landro paused for a moment. "I will explain that to-morrow. If you will excuse me, I will now return to my ship."

With that, Landro smiled at the PM and walked out to the small space car which silently rose to the main ship above.

Chapter 8

Upon the shuttle's departure, pandemonium broke out. Polly agreed to take a few questions but she was desperate to get away, to digest what had been said. To most of the questions, she could only say that they had heard as much as she had and that she knew no more. To the question, "What next?" she said she would return to Downing Street, talk to her advisers and leaders of other nations and be ready to talk to Landro tomorrow.

The TV and radio stations and Internet blogs were buzzing. University professors and experts on mythology were located and put on the air. Conspiracy theorists who had always believed that the Annunaki were real were exultant.

In the United States the president instructed his staff to get hold of the UK prime minister upon her return to Downing Street. In the meantime, he turned his attention to his advisers and in particular the chief of staff and the head of Space Command.

"Any ideas who this guy Landro is and why he is really here? Any tracers yet on his arrival? What do we know of the ship?"

General Carlos Ramirez, Chairman of the Joint Chiefs

of Staff, replied, "We know nothing more about the ship than we did before. We are not sure whether this is the only ship or whether there is a larger ship up there. Initial radar scans suggested something bigger but we have no sightings, either from Earth or from our satellites. The guys at Nellis say they think there will be another ship. They do not think this vessel is big enough for interstellar travel, assuming that it has come from Sirius as Landro said. And Nellis says they still think there is a sting in this – possibly their earlier discussions with us around Project Enterprise have triggered a reaction, although they had no idea how the Sirians might have known about that. Nellis are aware of the Grand Council but try to keep well below its radar."

"Will they help us militarily, if needed?"

"Not sure – we didn't specifically ask – but I wouldn't be confident."

An aide entered the room and announced, "I have the UK prime minister on the line, Mr President."

The president took the call. "Polly, hi, how are you? How does it feel to be the most famous woman in the world right now?"

"Great – I'm a politician after all! Not sure what to make of it all, to be honest. We can't find out any more about the ship than we did when it first arrived. In the meantime, I am gathering our experts on mythologies – the reference to the Annunaki and the fact that the vessel is called *Sumer* is a clear signal back to the Sumerian mythology. We're digging into that. I guess your people are too. Anything new your end?"

"No, nothing new here. I guess we will just wait for tomorrow's encounter. But find out more about this Grand Council, if you can."

The next day, the same events took place. This time, however, when Landro exited the vessel, another figure, also very tall but female, joined him. Equally dark-skinned with long silver hair, she was dressed in a similar but not identical tunic.

"Good morning, Prime Minister. Allow me to introduce my co-commander, Vendra. Vendra looks after all the technical aspects of this mission."

The PM looked surprised but quickly recovered. "You are welcome too, of course. Are you both able to say any more about your mission today?"

"I wish to do that at what you call the United Nations in three days' time. This should be enough time for all your leaders to get there. But I recognise that I need to present some credentials for you to accept my presence there...and here."

Vendra put down a small object. A screen emerged and displayed a picture.

"We have a message here from our chairman, and a background film about the council and the galaxy. As I show you this, it will simultaneously be transmitted on all the world's major TV stations, translated into the appropriate languages."

Before the PM could respond, the film began. First, a small hominid figure appeared, with a child's body but a big head and large teardrop eyes. He, she or it began to speak, with what appeared simultaneous translation, although there was a brief moment when the audience could hear a harsh staccato language with various clicks.

"I am Vrin, President and Chairman of the Grand Council. I am what you would call a Sirian. Commanders Landro and Vendra and the Sirian emissary Tzok have been sent to your planet at our request. The role of our council is to ensure the safety and health of our galaxy and of the individual star systems and worlds that make it up. Only worlds with interstellar travel are represented on the council. The commanders will explain their mission in more detail to the leaders of your world but I confirm again that they are there with our authority."

The dialogue stopped but then the film moved on to show the council conducting a meeting. Most attendees seemed to be represented by holograms and there were more life forms than would test the imagination of most science fiction writers. A fair scattering was hominid but there were insect forms, large, tentacle, marine-looking creatures and one that looked like a large bat.

Switching from the council, the film showed the night sky as seen from Sirius, with a small arrow indicating the Sun. The camera then panned back to Qrxa, showing a planet covered with buildings and ground and air traffic. There were oceans and some non-built-up areas. Next there appeared a huge off-world habitat with a space station and pictures of space vehicles of every size and shape docking and undocking. An elevator led down to the planet's surface. Then back to a picture of the Sun, and the camera sped through the universe towards it with close-ups of the various planets, before homing in on the Moon, where detailed pictures of the far side showed a spacecraft and various clearly artificial structures. Zooming out, the camera headed for Earth, showing details of the three space stations. Zooming back in, the camera moved slowly over a section of the southern United States before crossing the Atlantic and showing Hyde Park. With that, the film stopped.

"I hope that goes some way to confirming that my presence here is authorised and that it is appropriate for me to address your planet's leaders," said Landro.

"Thank you, Commander," said Polly. "I am sure you realise that there is a huge amount here for me, for us, to digest but let me talk to the secretary general of the UN and to my fellow leaders and I will let you know as soon as possible about you addressing us all. And who is the Sirian emissary Tzok, who was referred to?"

The commander looked slightly disappointed but quickly recovered. "Of course. I understand that. But speed is important and therefore if it is not deemed possible in the three days I proposed, I will broadcast live anyway, as we have done just now. Tzok is on board *Sumer* – you will meet him shortly. Now please excuse me."

And with that, Landro and Vendra left the tent, boarded the craft and returned to *Sumer*.

The PM hid how taken aback she felt. She thought her response had been totally reasonable. But then she reflected on the film and thought how technically backward he must regard them all, and yet he had the patience to indulge them.

She returned to Number 10 and spoke to her fellow leaders, starting with the president of the United States.

"I don't see why we should agree to let him address us at the UN on his timetable and his terms, Polly. He's come up with a glitzy film but how do we know if it is even genuine?"

"I thought it looked genuine, Steve. Talking about the film, what did you make of the pictures of the Moon, and why did the film pan over southern United States so slowly?"

"No idea, Polly. I've put my people on it. Incidentally, Polly, why the hell did he land in London?"

"I'll ask him but it's probably because he knew we wouldn't shoot him for illegal entry!"

"That's a cheap shot, Polly," said the president, laughing. He liked Polly and they got on well. "Let me know how your conversations with the others go, but I must say I'm not keen."

Polly continued her calls until late into the night. Some leaders were keen to accept; some felt it was a plot and if they were all to meet they risked being murdered. In some of the more theocratic states there was clearly a raging debate going on between the politicians and the religious leaders.

In the end a majority was willing to attend the UN in three days' time as Landro had requested, but several leaders said they would not attend, or would send a deputy.

Chapter 9

The next morning Polly left Downing Street with her private secretary, Bryony, and the deputy chief of the defence staff. As they set off, she commented how odd it was that despite this contact being so momentous, they had already established a routine.

At exactly 10.00am, the small craft landed once again, and Landro and Vendra emerged. The media were present outside the tent but they were not allowed inside. Anti-eavesdropping equipment had been installed.

Polly shook hands with Landro and Vendra. She noticed that this time Vendra was wearing a different-coloured uniform to Landro. They entered the tent. She summarised the outcome of her discussions and confirmed that the meeting would go ahead in three days' time as Landro had requested but that not everyone would be attending. Landro seemed to shrug but only said that that was fine.

Polly thought that this might be the moment to try to find out some more information. "I'd like to ask you some questions. Why did your film show the far side of the Moon and pan slowly across southern United States before ending up over Hyde Park?"

"I think your American colleagues should answer that," replied Landro, with a small laugh.

"Why did you come here to London?"

"Because I thought you would be less likely than some nations to open fire on our ship, pointless though that would have been, and that you would not seek to prevent full, real-time media coverage. Apart from going to New York to the UN, we will continue for the time being to base ourselves here when on Earth."

"So what are you going to do between now and the UN meeting?"

"Prepare," answered Landro, rather seriously. "There is much to cover and much to be done."

Vendra added, "But if you wish, you and your colleagues are welcome to visit *Sumer*. That may help convince you and your fellow leaders that we are not a hoax."

"When?"

"Now, if you like."

Ignoring the 'don't dream of it' comments from her security detail, the PM smiled and said she would be delighted.

Bryony, her private secretary, paled but stepped forward, as did the deputy chief. They could hear the cameras clicking as all three headed towards the small shuttle. Polly turned to the cameras, explaining that they had been invited to make a brief visit to Landro's spacecraft and that they had accepted.

They stepped into the shuttle. Chairs emerged from the floor and enfolded each of them – firmly but comfortably – and the vessel rose noiselessly upwards.

"How do you do that?" asked the deputy.

"Anti-gravity," explained Vendra. "We create a bubble around the vessel that harmonises with the Earth's gravity field. Altering and flexing the parameters of the bubble allows us to use the gravity field as an external propulsion system."

"Would you share that technology with us?" asked the deputy chief of the defence staff.

"Possibly one day…but a lot would need to happen first."

The shuttle docked with *Sumer*. The seats retracted and a hatch opened. The group walked through and found themselves in a small hold. Beyond that another door opened. A small, thin figure, with a greyish appearance, a large head and huge teardrop eyes, like Vrin, hurried through. In the background they could see two or three similar figures peering at them.

"Welcome," said the small figure, appearing to utilise a simultaneous translation device. "I am Tzok. I am the Sirian commander and representative on this mission."

The PM thought it would sound rather lame to say 'Hello', but 'Greetings' sounded like something from an early science fiction film and 'Good Morning' seemed quaintly formal. Finally, she settled on: "Hello, it is a pleasure and an honour to meet you, Commander Tzok. Should I or may I shake your hand?"

"We normally just raise our right hands in greeting." Tzok gave a small wave.

The deputy chief said, "I hope you don't mind me saying, but you and the council president look familiar, like the figures from…"

"Roswell," said Tzok. "Indeed, they were from Sirius."

"What were they doing here and how come they crashed, given your stupendous technology?"

"Overconfidence, I am embarrassed to say. They came through a portal too close to Earth, and the Earth's electromagnetic field was stronger than they thought. Their computer didn't harmonise their anti-gravity drive in time and consequently crashed."

"Did any of them survive?"

"One survived briefly but then succumbed to his injuries. It was never clear if those injuries came from the crash itself or from actions taken by those first on the scene. Sadly the Americans chose to hush the whole thing up and then tried to retro-develop the technology. They weren't very successful but of course it did prove to them that there was extra-terrestrial life, and they have been working on contacts with that ever since. That was why we showed Area 51 and Nellis Air Force Base at the end of the film."

"We wondered if that was why you panned so slowly over southern US. There are rumours that they have made contact…"

Tzok reflected and then said, "Not with us…not until now have we sought to make direct contact. That mission was a reconnaissance mission and those, mainly unmanned, have continued."

"So what are all the UFOs that get reported?"

"Most are the result of hysteria or natural phenomena. Some are top-secret planes developed by Earth countries, mainly the US, using the technology that they have either retro-engineered from Roswell or more recently that has been acquired from other non-Earth species. Some are also genuine non-Earth-origin visitors – you would be surprised at what has been going on at your planet and in your solar system over the millennia."

Polly looked at the deputy. "Are you aware of this? I wasn't. Only the usual conspiracy theories, which my sons share with me."

The deputy looked slightly shame-faced. "We knew that

Roswell was for real, not that the US shared very much apart from the fact that it was a UFO and that they had recovered bodies. As for the rest, we had our suspicions but no proof. The landing in the forest at Rendlesham is our best attested event but there was never any proof of what actually happened there."

Looking back at the Sirian and the two Sirian humans, he asked, "You mentioned portals – is that how you get here?"

"Yes. We use what we call subspace. Without that it would be impossible."

"Will you share this particular technology?"

"One day maybe, but not yet," replied Tzok.

They had arrived at an observation deck. Below, they could see the whole of London and the surrounding countryside.

"Would you care for some tea?" asked Landro.

"How surreal!" said Polly, laughing nervously. "I suppose you are going to ask if we would like Earl Grey or English Breakfast."

"Mm," said Landro, "I could try but I thought I would offer you a Sirian speciality."

He suddenly started to speak in a slightly harsh, staccato language. Almost immediately a hatch opened to one side and a small tray with four beakers emerged, floating gently towards the group. Vendra gave everyone a beaker before sipping from her own.

"Just to confirm that it isn't poison," she said, laughing.

The group from Earth looked slightly apprehensively at the beakers. The PM took a deep breath and sipped her tea. It had a strange flavour, quite unlike anything she had ever tasted, but it was not unpleasant.

"What do you call this in your language?" she asked, curious.

"Kvar," replied Vendra.

"Is your language still spoken on Earth?"

"No. We were a whole tribe that was removed by the Wei and traded. Therefore, there must have been very few left who spoke in our tongue."

After a few more exchanges, the PM and her colleagues made to leave, and Vendra escorted them to the shuttle.

Chapter 10

Polly arrived on time at the General Assembly three days later. Over the last seventy-two hours, she had had many more conversations with other governments and had also had time to catch up with her two sons, Harry aged fifteen and Mark aged thirteen. Camping out on the top floor of Number 10, the boys had watched agog as their mother met the visitors from Sirius and they had wanted to talk all about it with her. She had no more answers to their questions than she had had with the media.

"This is so cool!" exclaimed Mark. "I can't believe my mum is the first person to meet an alien. Everyone at school is asking us about it."

"I think he is here to help us," said Harry.

"I hope you're right," said Polly. "I really hope you're right." Polly looked fondly at the two boys and gave them a hug. It was difficult for them having their mother as prime minister, more so since she and her husband had separated and then divorced years earlier.

Polly looked round the auditorium. The chairman of the assembly, supported by his staff, was presiding but he was not

51

currently in the room, having gone with the UN secretary general to await Landro. About two thirds of the countries were represented by their leaders, several others by their ambassadors and a few by their deputies. She noted that the US president was absent, but the US ambassador, John Redlan, was attending in his place.

She had passed on Tzok's comments about the Roswell crash to Steve but he had said very little, limiting himself to an enigmatic comment that this was all very difficult.

A brief commotion at the door and Landro, the chairman and the secretary general appeared. They walked to the rostrum, where a suitably high microphone had been placed. The chairman introduced Landro.

"Thank you, Mr Chairman. As you heard three days ago, I have been asked to come to this planet at the request of the Grand Council and its president, Chairman Vrin. The council has many concerns about this planet, your planet, which has led to this mission." Landro paused.

The chamber was silent.

"To those looking at your planet from the outside, the humans of Earth look like a pestilence and an infestation. You are the most evolved species – helped admittedly by the Wei's genetic experiments – but rather than recognising the responsibility that comes with that to care for other life forms and for the planet as a whole, you have systematically pillaged the planet's resources and subdued or exterminated all other species.

"Not only do you seek to subdue or exterminate other species but you also regularly fight each other and seek to exterminate or enslave parts of your own species. There is very little meaningful care or compassion for those members of the human race who do not have enough to eat, or who live under appalling conditions.

"The likelihood is therefore that given the track you are on you will succeed in exterminating yourselves. The planet will cease to provide what you need. Indeed, your current lifestyle requires at least three planets to be sustainable. On the current track its atmosphere will become intolerable for humans.

"None of this would matter except for two things: firstly, this planet is, or at least was, a jewel in the universe. It is in pain. We cannot allow this planet to be destroyed by you. Moreover the planet is beginning to take things into its own hands. Look at the earthquakes, volcanic eruptions and extreme climate events that keep happening.

"Secondly, you have ambitions to become a spacefaring race. Because of discussions that certain governments are having with other spacefaring species, this opportunity is closer than you think. For the council, the idea of more humans from this planet seeking to spread your appalling track record is not a risk that can be taken, and we will prevent this until you can show that you are fit to join the galactic community.

"So," and here Landro paused again and looked around him, "there needs to be a change, a drastic and total change. You, all of you, need to change, immediately. You must stop taking all of the natural resources of the planet and using them so wastefully. You must learn to live off what the planet can produce on a sustainable basis.

"You must reduce your population radically and restore areas to the other species on this planet – animals and plants – where there is no threat from humans. You will cease your discussions about interstellar travel with other off-world species. This will not be allowed to continue.

"I will return in six months, at which time you will present your plans for the changes needed. If the plans are acceptable, you will implement them." Then, speaking very slowly, in his deep, sonorous voice, he added, "If they are not acceptable, we will take our own proposals to the council for an imposed solution. It is up to you."

Landro stopped, turned to the chairman, bowed slightly and walked out of the door.

"Stop him!" cried the US ambassador.

The security guards looked doubtful. One stepped tentatively forward but he could not get closer than a couple of metres to Landro, who seemed to have activated a shield. He walked out of the building and into the small shuttle which rose quickly to *Sumer*, sitting stationary over the river. *Sumer* rose effortlessly upwards, rapidly disappearing from view.

Back in the chamber there was uproar. The US ambassador spoke first.

"I will speak to the president but in my view that is outrageous. We will not be threatened in that way and we will defend ourselves against anything that is thrown at us."

The Russian ambassador spoke in similar terms.

The Chinese president asked, "What did the visitor mean when he referred to contact with other spacefaring peoples?" He looked pointedly at the American and Russian delegations.

"We have no idea what he meant by that," replied the US ambassador.

Polly had been gathering her thoughts and now spoke. "I agree that we need to prepare to defend ourselves, but the fact is that what he says is correct. If he means what he says about imposing a solution, then I think we need to reflect on how we deal with infestations here. I have a chilling feeling that if we do not offer some kind of solution when he returns, he may well impose a solution which excludes us humans on Earth. As he said, that would not be the end of humanity since there are other humans in the galaxy – it would just be the end of us."

She was silent for a moment.

"I suggest we take on his challenge and that we urgently look at options, including the most drastic. It is not as if we do not know what the issues are or that we have not been looking for solutions. Let us set up a working group chaired by the secretary general. Until then we need to stay in permanent session."

The discussions continued with increasing rancour and pandemonium. A number of countries accused the West of having brought this upon the Earth because of their greed and materialistic values. Several suggested they should all pray. But enough nations agreed that the Earth needed to prepare itself for a battle. There were several stirring speeches declaring that if they were going to be destroyed, they would go down fighting. Many countries continued to question the references to other alien contacts. Essentially, enough countries backed the UK proposal for a working group to develop a plan that would address Landro's points.

Chapter 11

Back on *Sumer*, Landro, Vendra and Tzok were watching the debate with interest.

"A pretty predictable reaction," said Vendra. "We need to stay and monitor what happens."

"If they decided to defend the planet, could they do it successfully?" asked Landro.

"Not on their own," replied Vendra, "and I doubt that the Arisi that we know of at Nellis would bring in their own forces. We are not aware that the Americans are talking to anyone else."

"What about the US base on the Moon?" Landro continued.

"There is some advanced technology there that has not been shared with other nations."

"Why are the Arisi helping the Americans and what is in it for them?"

"Well," replied Vendra, "they are hardly a peaceful race themselves and they probably see the violent instincts of Earth's humans as something they can harness and manage for their own ends – perhaps use them as shock troops. They will feel strong enough to defend themselves, and the Arisi have always thrived on chaos. The current galactic order doesn't suit them at all. They still smart from the constraints that the council tried to put on them decades ago."

"Would they challenge the council?"

"I don't believe that they would but just as we have found them hiding here they have probably been hiding elsewhere, stirring things up and developing their technologies. We are very advanced but we are still developing new technologies ourselves so who is to say that others are not doing the same thing?" pointed out Tzok, who had been silent up till now.

"Let us check out the Moon base first more closely," suggested Landro, "and then perhaps check out some of the other planets. But before we go I need to speak to Polly again."

"She's 'Polly' now, is she?" said Vendra, laughing.

Landro gave her a look, and then delivered instructions to the ship.

Chapter 12

In Washington, the US president had summoned his advisers.

"So how much more do we know? What do we think he can do? How realistic is it for us to fight this guy Landro and his ship? We saw the galactic council video but that could have been a simulation. Maybe he is just trying to scam us."

The head of Space Command replied, "Well, we know that a race that looks like the president of the council and Tzok exists because we had the bodies from Roswell. We know that the bits of the ship that we recovered from Roswell were very sophisticated. We never managed to cut through the pieces of the hull fabric, never mind piece together the few surviving pieces of the engine system. We know because of what we have seen the aliens at Nellis use that anti-gravity drives exist and, indeed, they have let us use one of their ships to set up our base on the far side of the Moon. They have not, however, shared that technology with us.

"We know the Nellis aliens have weapons that are superior to ours and presumably the Sirians do as well. Apart from some help with laser technology, they have also been giving us some technology for plasma-weapons technology.

This has been tested on the Moon and is a step up from anything anyone else has. Whether it would be enough to penetrate the Sirian shield that Landro referred to when he first arrived, is unknown. However, basic physics tells us that an energy shield must drain energy when it is being utilised and any one ship must have less capacity than the resources of a planet, if we could just work out how to harness that."

"What do we actually call the aliens at Nellis, apart from 'the aliens at Nellis'?" asked the president.

"Everyone calls them the Tall Whites," replied the head of Space Command.

"Well, have you talked to these Tall Whites directly or just through our guys at Nellis?"

"I spoke via video conference yesterday and again immediately after the UN speech. I asked how helpful to us they could be if it came to a showdown. Their reply was that they valued their contact with us, valued the base that we had given them at Nellis and would not want to see us destroyed. However, they did not specify what they would or could do to help us."

"And Project Enterprise?"

"That is still going strong. We have been asking them for years to let us see their home world and other worlds, and they now seem to be prepared to allow a small group, including some military, do just that. They have subspace travel, like Landro claims he has, so the time implications are very small."

"I am guessing that we should not share any of this. I am getting a lot of pressure from Polly for more detail, and you saw the other questions that came up after the UN speech."

"Perhaps we should confirm Roswell and the discovery of the alien bodies. That should be sufficient for the time being, and despite our efforts there is so much in the public domain about that, it wouldn't come as a surprise. But I wouldn't say anything about the Tall Whites or the Moon base."

"Sounds sensible," agreed the president. "Incidentally, what do the Tall Whites call themselves?"

"It's something unpronounceable. The best we've managed to translate it is as Orsi. The only thing we know for sure is that they are from the Draco system."

Back in London, Polly had just finished her meeting with the small Cabinet group that she had set up to deal with the Landro visit. As well as senior ministers, it included her most senior military, a couple of eminent archaeologists and mythologists, who were still sifting for clues about what Landro had said about the Wei, and an eminent anthropologist. Regarding the Wei, the archaeologists were excited to be able to see threads that previously only conspiracy theorists had taken seriously that would support Landro's description, such as the remains of cities in the Indus valley which looked like they had been destroyed in a nuclear attack.

The military had little to add to what the Americans already knew. They said that they had been pressing the United States for details of other alien contacts but, apart from confirming the Roswell incident, they were being very guarded. They did, however, report that the president was proposing to address the nation regarding Landro's speech, and he would include Roswell.

"I should speak to the country as well," said Polly.

She spent the rest of the afternoon going through what she should say with her advisers, and that evening she went on TV and the radio:

"You will all have been following recent events with

the same fascination as I have. You will all have heard and probably seen the speech that Commander Landro made at the UN.

"This contact is a momentous event for our planet and for humanity. We are privileged that it has happened in our lifetime. It is extraordinary to know for certain that we are not alone in this universe and even more extraordinary to discover that there are other humans out there.

"The commander laid down a very real challenge to us. I believe his judgement on us is harsh. Nevertheless he raises genuine issues where we have struggled to get consensus and where we now must now do so. I'd like to think that this contact is just the sort of external catalyst that we needed for us to work together, not just in this country but across the world. Our differences and squabbles look very small in the context of the bigger universe, of which we are now apparently a part…a very small part admittedly, but a part nonetheless.

"I know that many of you will be frightened for the future. I have met and spoken with the commander more than anyone else. I may be wrong but I do not believe he has any more wish to destroy us than we have to destroy ourselves. He is not an alien, but a human, and shares, I believe, a common humanity with us. I want us to draw on his help and support and not fight him.

"That said, we will not hesitate to defend ourselves if the worst comes to the worst. But I do not believe it will.

"So please stay calm. I will speak to you regularly as we develop our plans and response for when the commander returns in six months. God bless us all and look after us."

Polly returned to Downing Street and was relaxing with a hot drink when her personal mobile pinged. It was a text message from an unknown number.

Landro here — I will call you in a minute.

Before she could get over the surprise of how he had her number, the phone rang.

"Good speech tonight, if I may say so. You are right about the common humanity. That surprised me — the other humans I have met have all been travellers, aware of the sheer scale of the universe and its history, and we shared the same language even if it has evolved differently on different planets. But I am aware of a common feeling with the humans I have met here. I do not want it to come to a fight either, but if you humans on Earth cannot change your ways, radically and quickly, then I will intervene. This planet is a living being, Polly, and it is in pain. Of more concern than my actions, may be its actions. It will defend itself if the threat becomes too much, and in some ways it already is. I have come here before that becomes much worse.

"I will also, as I said, make sure that Earth's humans do not leave this solar system. So yes, I hope we don't end up with a fight but I will not shrink from it if it does."

"Thank you for your comment on my speech, Landro. This is a big challenge for us. But why are you ringing me and telling me this? Also, where are you? I thought you were heading off for six months."

"I said I would return to the UN in six months. And where am I? Out there, as you said in your speech. And why am I calling you? Perhaps the common humanity — I wanted to. You are the human here with whom I have had the most contact. Despite all our research and implants, direct conversation tells me more. And I hope you can work with others who think like you to make progress on what I asked at the UN."

Polly thought for a moment. "I am happy to meet again if that would help. Can we?"

"Of course, but not now."

"You called me. Can I call you if need be?"

There was a moment's silence before Landro replied, "I do not see why not. I will set that up and send you a number."

With that, the call ended.

Polly decided she needed a small brandy. What a strange call, she thought. Why would he ring her? She sent a message to Bryony, her private secretary, briefly telling her what had happened.

As she sat back and sipped her drink, she thought about Landro. She wondered what sort of man he really was. On his first appearance, he had seemed quite warm. However, at the UN, he had been very forthright and, indeed, she felt he could be totally ruthless. This evening's call to her was odd. His message was very formal, yet he had rung her out of the blue.

Ever since the divorce eight years ago, Polly had dedicated herself totally to her work. She had been too busy to think about relationships. She found herself thinking about that now. Then she asked herself why she was even thinking about that. A phone call from Landro didn't create a relationship. Indeed, the idea was absurd! But then why had he rung her? And he had promised a number. Just at that moment her phone buzzed again, and there was a number, from Landro. She hesitated and then texted.

Thank you, and thank you for your call, Polly.

She hesitated again before pressing the send button. Four minutes later, her phone buzzed.

My pleasure.

She smiled and finished her drink.

Aboard *Touching the Heavens* where they had docked a couple of hours previously, Vendra raised her eyebrows when Landro told her of the call and why he had rung.

"That is a pretty feeble justification. And don't build too close a relationship. Don't forget, you may be asked to destroy them all."

"I don't want to think about that. I am hoping that Polly can harness the energies that are there to come up with the radical solutions needed. They are all intelligent enough but I don't know whether they can get agreement. And I do worry about the Arisi and what they may do. Anyway, let's go travelling."

With that, the ship, fully cloaked, moved slowly towards the Moon.

"The President of the United States", said the announcer with all the gravity she could muster.

The president appeared on the screen, sitting in the Oval Office.

"My fellow Americans, you will all have been following the extraordinary events of recent days, most recently the alien Landro's speech to the United Nations. Let me make this clear: we will not be browbeaten or threatened, and not for the first time, the United States of America stands ready to defend humanity. We are making our preparations now, with our allies, and if the aliens continue with their threats, we will fight and destroy them when they return.

"I wish to address one issue which arose at the UN and which has been in the papers since, and that is the question of previous alien contact. I acknowledge to you today that we have had alien contact in the past, when an alien spacecraft crashed at Roswell. We recovered two bodies and the remains of their spacecraft. For many decades the government denied there had been any contact and at the time there were good reasons for that: The Cold War was starting, and it was considered to be in the best interests of all Americans not to share this. It has, I accept, been kept secret for longer than necessary. General Tevez of Space Command will provide more details after I have spoken.

"In the meantime, I urge you all to remain calm and carry on with your normal business. The world is not ending, and as I said earlier we are well able to defend ourselves if it came to that. However, I do not believe that it will. God Bless you all, and God Bless America!"

Chapter 13

Vendra kept the ship cloaked as it edged towards the far side of the Moon. Long-range scanners soon picked up a number of artificial structures, including what looked like a launch site. A couple of miles away there was also a site which resembled a weapons-testing site. A small vehicle was moving slowly away, back towards the main complex.

"I doubt that is a remnant of the Wei – perhaps it is the Arisi," said Landro.

"Hang on a moment, said Vendra. "Let me focus here." She homed in on a large stars and stripes design.

"But how did the Americans get here? Perhaps the Arisi helped them. I wonder what it is they're testing at the weapons range."

"Looking at the scorch marks, I would say it is either lasers or possibly plasma cannon. We haven't come across any details of those before but we know the Arisi have them so it looks like they're sharing."

"Does that pose a problem for us?"

"Not if our shields hold," said Vendra.

"I would love to take them out now," said Landro, "but I suppose that would be inappropriate."

"It would," said Tzok, firmly.

Very slowly, the ship edged away and out of the sight line.

"I have an idea," said Landro.

Polly's mobile phone rang just as she was drying her hair. Her initial irritation disappeared when she saw the number.

"Landro? This is a surprise. Good to hear from you." Polly bit her lip. That sounded a bit too enthusiastic and not prime ministerial enough.

"Polly, I am sending you a photograph of the far side of the Moon plus some transcripts of coded messages. These show the extent of the American presence on the Moon. I trust you to use them carefully when you ask the US president about them. I have enlarged the area that shows the US flag."

"I suppose I should be shocked but I am not totally surprised. I thought there might be more. The president has been very coy recently about what the US is up to, although he has now come clean about Roswell. But on the Moon? That is a real surprise. How did they get there?"

"Probably anti-gravity drives. And, you could ask him about what is going on at Nellis Air Force Base as well. Let me know how you get on."

"Thank you for all of this...but why are you telling me? And where are you?"

"I'm telling you because you seem to be focusing on the problem and the challenge I laid down, and I trust you to bring everyone behind you. As for where I am... I'm still out there. Take care, Polly, and good night."

Landro was pensive for a moment as he rang off. Then he caught Vendra's sardonic grin.

"You always were one for the ladies, weren't you?"

"It's not like that." Landro grunted and headed out.

Tzok looked quizzically after him. "There are many things that I do not understand about humans," he said to Vendra, "and the computer does not help."

Vendra laughed and then became serious. "It's difficult to explain, Tzok. Human emotions are both one of our greatest gifts and one of our biggest liabilities. That is why it is good working around you Sirians – you never seem to get distracted."

"Maybe we can develop a corrective implant," said Tzok.

Vendra raised her eyebrows. "But then we wouldn't be human, would we?"

Tzok grunted in response.

Polly was not sure what to do with the information Landro had given her. She summoned the close team who were advising her and after a deep breath she placed the pictures on the table.

The chief of the defence staff examined them and then asked where she had got them.

"Landro sent them to me." She described her conversation. "I believe they are genuine."

The chief paused for a moment and then cautioned, "You need to be careful, Prime Minister, with these contacts. Don't lose sight of the fact that you are talking to aliens, even if they are human, and we do not know what their intentions are.

"As for the photos, we had our suspicions, but the Americans have never shared this with us. Nor, so far as we know, have they shared this with anyone else. Do we go public or do you talk to the president and tell him you might go public unless he does?"

"I'll call the president."

*

"Prime Minister, I have the president on the line for you."

"What can I do for you, Polly?" said the president, with what she felt was forced good humour.

"It was good to hear you telling everyone about Roswell. I think it would be a good thing if you were to go further and tell everyone about what has been happening at Nellis and what you've been doing on the far side of the Moon."

There was a moment's silence.

"Good joke, Polly. There's nothing to tell."

"Steve, you know there is, and it would be so much better coming from you than us."

"This is ridiculous, Polly. Who would believe you?"

"They would believe the pictures and the transmissions that I have in my possession."

"Have you been spying on us?"

"As it happens, no. But someone else has, and we have that intelligence."

"This is such crap, Polly." With that, the president hung up.

Half an hour later, the president was surrounded by his advisers. "How the hell do the Brits know this stuff?" he demanded.

"We don't know that they do know. They might just be bluffing," said General Tevez.

At that moment, an assistant ran in and handed a package to the president.

He opened it and paled. The message read: "To help your discussions. Polly." The contents were the pictures of the Moon base and transcripts of various transmissions.

"Shit!" shouted the general. "How the hell did they get those? As far as we know there are no non-US assets up there that could obtain these."

"Landro," guessed the president. "He has been buddying up to Polly ever since he made contact, and she was the one who gave his message any real airtime at the UN." He reflected a moment. "But in a sense it doesn't matter how she got them. We just need to think about what to do. At least she warned us that she had this rather than going straight to the UN. I guess the 'special relationship' that the Brits keep going on about isn't totally dead," he said, slightly sarcastically.

Chapter 14

As six months passed, people had to keep reminding themselves of the extraordinary visit from Landro. Even some non-space or alien-related headlines started to appear again. People had generally remained calm and continued much as normal. Archaeologists were busier than ever, revisiting their old assumptions and discovering just how much they had managed to misinterpret. Now they knew the answer, several mysteries suddenly appeared so much less mysterious. Still, they all wanted to have a chance to get some questions to Landro, which they were sure he could answer.

Polly, meanwhile, was trying to get a team together at the UN to look at Landro's challenge. It was not easy; several nations refused to have anything to do with it, and always the arguments raged about whose fault the state of the planet was. It didn't matter how often Polly said that it didn't really matter whose fault it was if the whole of humankind was at risk, and that they should focus on finding a solution. However, she did manage to bring together a team of scientists and political advisers who reported on a weekly basis to her and a number of other political representatives. The options had to be radical, given what was in effect Landro's ultimatum.

First up was the creation of much larger national parks from which most humans would be excluded – large areas of Russia, Africa, northern Scandinavia, the Antarctic, the Amazon delta (with a proposal to leave the existing indigenous tribes there). Cutting the population was the difficult issue, as was the enforced migration that would follow the creation of human-free areas. Extreme birth control was the only way to drastically reduce numbers over say, 100 years. But how to enforce that and how to manage the drastic economic impacts of a radically shrinking population? Polly despaired of coming up with anything coherent.

The United States had sent some scientists and a political observer along to Polly's group but the president's view was that Polly was wasting her time. Their focus was on defence. He found support from Russia and China, and the three nations became unlikely collaborators. It also became clear that both Russia and China had more assets in space than the United States had realised, albeit, not so far as they could tell, anything similar to their plasma cannon.

Space Command had asked the Tall Whites for more help with their weaponry. In particular they wanted to know how to pierce the shields of Landro's spacecraft.

The president met his advisers to discuss this. "So, any progress? Will they help us?"

"They would like to," replied General Tevez, "but it is also clear that they have had their run-ins with the galactic council, and are wary of having any more. Their approach seems to be to stay off the council's radar. We of course cannot do that. They did confirm our point that a planet-based weapons system should always be able to drain the shields of any attacking ship but there are limitations to our energy systems. To sustain the plasma cannon we need far more energy generation than we currently have, and we clearly don't have time to build much more capacity. The biggest problem, of course, is that we don't really know what energy sources are available to Landro. The scientists looking at how he got here and, indeed, how the Tall Whites get around say that clearly, they are accessing other forms of energy than we are. They talked of scalar energy."

"What's that?" asked the president.

"Well, we know about it. A guy called Tesla did a lot of work on it in the late nineteenth century but in the end industry went with the electro-magnetic energy sources that we now use."

"Why?"

"Simple. More money in it for industry. Tesla proposed giving his energy away so no one wanted to invest in it."

The president raised his eyebrows in disbelief.

"The Russians, however, have continued their research into this scalar energy. We believe they have been developing some weaponry harnessing it and the laws of quantum physics to develop a type of explosive device which can be exploded in one location, but the impact of the blast channelled somewhere else. We have our suspicions that one or two seismic events may have been triggered as a result of testing of these weapons. Perhaps you could ask President Andrinov…"

The conversation with President Andrinov took place shortly afterwards, whereby the Russians initially denied that they had been developing any such weapons and instead started to ask about the US capability with plasma cannon and about Moon bases.

The US president took a deep breath. "President Andrinov, Yuri, the future of our planet may be at stake here, and we need to cooperate, just as we did once before in World War II. So, yes, I am prepared to confirm that we have been developing a plasma cannon and that the prototype has been tested on the far side of the Moon where we have established a base."

President Andrinov sounded thoughtful as he replied, "I could make the point that your weapons in space and presence on the Moon are in direct contradiction to many international treaties. However, I recognise that we may need to work together so I suggest that your military scientists meet with mine as soon as possible."

Aboard *Touching the Heavens*, Landro and Vendra listened to the call.

"If the Russians really have been developing scalar energy weapons, then we need to be very careful," said Landro. "Even with our shield systems, we will need to maintain a very high level of alert."

Landro, Vendra and Tzok proceeded to discuss how they should spend the remainder of the six months. They decided to do a more thorough survey of the solar system for three months and then return to Qrxa to brief Vrin and the council.

Chapter 15

Six months later, the UN reconvened. Landro had reconfirmed the date and time and explained that *Sumer* would hover over the Hudson River and that he would drop down to the UN building in the capsule.

The day arrived. The delegates were present and huge TV screens showed *Sumer* coming into view, high above the city. It hovered at around 500 feet, and the small shuttle detached itself from the underside. Suddenly there was a searing flash of light and the shuttle and *Sumer* were briefly illuminated before they seemed to explode into a million pieces.

Everyone gasped in horror. Polly was rooted to the spot, unable to comprehend what she had just witnessed.

Suddenly attention switched to the dais where presidents McIerney and Andrinov now appeared.

The US president was the first to speak. "Mr Secretary General, Presidents, Prime Ministers, Ambassadors, Delegates. Our ambassador said when we last met here that we, the US, would not be threatened and that we would meet force with force. We have worked with our Russian allies to defend this planet against the threats posed by the Sirian, and what you have seen is our response to his threats. These aliens should not underestimate our ability to defend ourselves."

Polly was about to speak when her phone buzzed. The text read:

If you speak, know that I am fine and that I will be arriving shortly. Landro.

Polly was speechless. She had just witnessed the destruction of the craft with her own eyes, yet she felt that Landro was somehow alive.

The Chinese deputy president had just finished speaking in support of the joint US and Russian action.

It was Polly's turn. "I am appalled by what has happened and what the consequences might be. For the US and Russia to act together without consultation even with their close allies is unacceptable."

Before she could continue, the doors swung open and Landro entered. He shimmered as he walked, and Polly realised that he must have a protective shield around him. He strode to the dais.

"I agree that this action is unacceptable. It is also extremely foolish. As I speak, your US base on the Moon is being neutralised and the source in Russia of the weapon with which my craft was attacked has also been destroyed. You may feel threatened by me and my visit but I have been offering you a chance to show that you can respond to the challenge I laid down. What you have done instead is demonstrate the very behaviour which concerned the council and which brought me here in the first place."

The presidents of Russia and the United States rose from their seats in unison.

"Sit down!" barked Landro. He strode across the chamber to where the US president sat. "You will come with me."

Several of the US entourage tried to get between Landro and the president but they found themselves unable to move, as did the president himself. When Landro reached him, it was as if the shimmer of Landro's suit enveloped the president. Suddenly a tiny beam of light came through the roof and shone on the floor of the assembly chamber. It widened, pulverising the ceiling around, and a gentle haze of dust drifted downwards, settling on all those nearby. Everyone watched, transfixed. Through the hole came the small shuttle. It hovered close to Landro and the president. Landro dragged the president after him into the craft. It rose through the hole to *Sumer*, which in turn ascended and disappeared from view.

After an initial buzz and some brief bilateral exchanges everyone headed for the exit, fearing an attack was imminent. The building quickly emptied. Miraculously no one had been seriously injured. It was as if the hole had been carefully created to avoid any casualties.

Polly and the British ambassador headed back to the British UN embassy building.

"Give me a moment on my own," she said. She looked at the text message. What the hell was going on?

It had been an hour since the text. She took a deep breath and called the number Landro had given her. To her amazement, he answered.

"What is happening?" she cried. "How did you survive? What have you done with the US president? And what happens next?"

"He is cooling down in a cabin here. Vendra and Tzok are with him. I will talk to him later. He is in a state of shock.

"As for the explosion. Well, the attack was real but Vendra managed to simulate the appearance of *Sumer* and the shuttle using the tractor beam and then simulated the explosion. We were nowhere near it. She is pleased that the simulation was so effective.

"And as for what next, I don't yet know. I know that you have been working on your plans but that you have had very little cooperation from the US and Russia (you now know why) and that you have been unable to reach an agreement. I am actually worried about consequences that are out of my control.

"I am sorry, I need to go. I will talk to you again soon."

And with that, the call ended.

Polly spoke to the ambassador and they agreed it was imperative the UN reconvened immediately. The ambassador rushed away to confer with allies and with the secretary general.

Chapter 16

A hotel close to the UN building made its ballroom available for the presidents, prime ministers, ambassadors and other delegates to meet later the same day. The normal protocols on translation and other such matters were set aside as they sat down. The Russian president was the first to speak.

"It is clear that we are now in a state of war. I confirm that our facilities in Siberia where the weapon that we used on *Sumer* was based have suffered heavy damage. We are now on full alert and are ready to confront whatever forces the enemy puts against us."

The US vice president was about to stand, but the Russian president's words had so infuriated Polly that she jumped up and spoke before another word could be uttered.

"We are only at war because of the reckless and foolish trilateral action taken by the US, Russia and China without any consultation whatsoever with any other countries, countries that should have been consulted when the future of our entire Earth is at risk. What were you thinking? You are proving to Landro and his council that mankind is as foolish and unworthy as they all clearly believe. Our efforts to find a peaceful response to his challenge now look like an excuse to give us time to launch an attack. We must contact him as a matter of urgency, tell him that this action was not supported by the majority of people on Earth and try to get back to some sort of discussion and negotiation. We also need to hear from the US, Russia and China about their off-world bases and their contacts with other alien races – what was the purpose of this and why was that information not shared?"

Her words were greeted with warm applause.

The US vice president then stood. "You need to decide, Prime Minister Hawkins, whether you are on the side of your fellow humans on this planet or on the side of this alien human about whom we know nothing. We don't even know if he is really human. Your words are misjudged. Things are much more complicated than you understand. The United States will, like Russia, go on to full military readiness and we will fight on. We intend to preserve the self-determination of our planet and we will not be dictated to."

The anger in the room towards him and the Russians was palpable. He left in a hurry, promising that he would return shortly.

Back at the White House, the vice president, Tom Peterson, was hurriedly sworn in as acting president. He gathered his advisers around him. The head of United States Space Command confirmed the loss of the Moon base test facilities. The base itself was still in contact and the general there advised how the test facilities had been destroyed by some sort of energy weapon. The acting president turned on the general and asked why the defences had not been activated. The general prevaricated a while but eventually it became clear that because the tests were for a weapon that could be used against other countries on Earth, they had not felt the need to have anything but the most basic defences at the base. The general added that one notable thing was that the Tall White ship which was near the test site had been completely untouched. It wasn't clear if this had been done deliberately by Landro or if the Tall Whites had strong enough shields of their own.

"I need to meet these guys!" shouted the acting president. "Fix it!"

Meanwhile, Polly had also left the meeting and was back at the British embassy with the ambassador. She was shaking; she was so angry and upset.

"What is it with the Russians and the Americans? How do they not see that they cannot possibly win this? They don't know anything about Landro, apart from what he has told us. Saying we are at war is crazy. What are they going to attack? They can't even see his ship!"

"You have seen his ship," said the ambassador. "You have his trust. You could ask to meet him on his ship and leave a tracker on it."

Polly stared at him, appalled and speechless. She left the room and went to her bedroom.

She had only been there a short while when the phone rang and her private secretary advised her to turn on the television. She watched in horror the breaking news of an earthquake off the coast of Japan and the subsequent huge tsunamis. She had barely had a chance to absorb this disaster before the next piece of breaking news came through: there had been a huge earthquake on the San Andreas fault. First indications were that both quakes were above 9.5 on the Richter scale, which meant that they were stronger than any previously known earthquakes.

Another call advised that the UN were meeting again. Polly and the ambassador headed back to the hotel.

The Russian ambassador spoke first.

"It is clear that these earthquakes are not coincidences but acts of war. I have also to inform you that the plane carrying our president back to Russia has disappeared. Shortly after it left New York, the pilot reported that he was no longer in control of the plane and that it was being forced upwards. We have had no further contact with the pilot or with our president. We have to assume that this is the work of the Sirians. It proves that we were right to attack. We are facing a ruthless enemy and we must all prepare ourselves. I have spoken with my colleagues from the US and China and we agree that we will continue to work together in this fight."

With that, he left his seat and the US ambassador and the Chinese presidents left theirs.

Polly was about to stand, when the French president rose. Aurelie Malmaison had said little in the previous debates, despite France being on the security council.

"These disasters and events are not, I am sure, coincidences but I think we are being too hasty if we blame Landro. He told us when he first came here that the planet might take things into its own hands. None of us asked about that at the time but maybe that is what is happening."

She added, with unmasked disdain in her voice, "I am deeply concerned that the alpha male responses of our American, Russian and Chinese leaders may be the worst way to go forward, and that engaging the brain rather than other parts of the anatomy might be a better way forward." She turned and smiled at Polly. "Prime Minister Hawkins, Polly, you have had the most contact with Landro. Might you try to talk to him again?"

Polly was grateful for the vote of confidence from Aurelie and confirmed that she would try. The two women left the chamber.

Polly did not know Aurelie very well but had met her a handful of times over the years and had always been impressed by her common sense. She was less outgoing than many of her peers and did not seek the limelight. Nevertheless her practical and sensible attitude and naturally quiet authority meant that she was now a leading light in the EU. Polly admired her sure-footedness. She also admired Aurelie's immaculate dress sense and her petite figure, both of which left Polly feeling rather inadequate.

"You know, Polly," Aurelie said in her fluent but heavily accented English, "I think it is time for *les femmes* to get a grip on this. There is too much male testosterone flying around among our colleagues and it will end badly. It is clear that you have already built a relationship with Landro and it can only help that you are tall and good-looking. He finds you attractive. We must use that to our advantage."

Polly was taken aback. She was delighted to hear Aurelie say that she was good-looking yet taken aback at the sexist approach that Aurelie seemed to be proposing. It seemed totally inappropriate for her, as prime minister, to even think of such things. Nevertheless, she flushed slightly at the thought that Landro might find her attractive.

Aurelie saw her expression and laughed. "Do not pretend, Polly, that you do not understand me or know what I am talking about. You use your height and presence to overawe men as a modern-day Diana. I have seen you. I often wish I was as tall as you. But I am not and so I approach men differently. However, in this case, being tall has a different benefit since you are the only woman who is not totally dwarfed by Landro." She added with a laugh, "It is good to know that even men from another planet are so predictable!"

Polly was still rather flustered but after further discussion they parted company and went their separate ways.

Reports on the two earthquakes were shocking. Japan's east coast had been pummelled by tsunamis, and there was huge concern over the fate of the nuclear power stations there. Although it was now well over twenty-five years since the Fukushima Daiichi disaster, and additional precautions against further meltdowns had been made, the scale of this earthquake was such that some of the stations appeared to have been over-whelmed.

The networks, however, were focusing much more on the California earthquake, which had hit with unprecedented ferocity and, alarmingly, seemed to be causing the plate on which San Francisco and its adjacent coastline sat to disappear into the Pacific. The rescue services were working flat out but the destruction was total and the death toll was predicted to be in the millions.

Polly sat with her staff and the ambassador, as they all stared at the television, appalled at the events unfolding.

"We must get a message to both the US and Japanese governments offering all and any help they may need. I will speak as soon as possible to the vice president."

Needless to say the vice president was engaged but Polly left a message, and did the same with the Japanese premier. She decided that she needed to get to London as soon as possible. Once the necessary travel arrangements had been made, she departed.

Chapter 17

Landro had been equally shocked by the pictures of the earthquakes, particularly the one in California. He had been watching *Sumer*'s tractor beam bringing the plane carrying the Russian president up to *Sumer*, where it had docked. The Russian president and his entourage had been moved to *Sumer*, and the president had been separated from the others.

Sumer moved rapidly to dock with *Touching the Heavens*. The whole operation had taken less than an hour when President Andrinov found himself in front of Landro and Vendra.

"This is an outrage!" he spluttered. "I demand that you release me and everyone on my plane immediately."

"It is no less an outrage than your unprovoked attack on my ship, which was clearly intended to kill not just me but everyone on board," replied Landro. "You will stay here with me and your comrade-in-arms, the US president. The plane and the others on board will be returned to Moscow. The plane's electronics were damaged by the tractor beam, which means we will have to make a detour to Russia."

Landro fetched the US president who was still swearing, and showed him the feed.

"My God, Yuri, have they got you too?" said Steve to the Russian president.

The Russian president said something in Russian.

Vendra handed each president a small device which she explained would help them understand each other.

Having looked at the feed from the TV channels about the two earthquakes, Steve turned on Landro.

"You will pay for this. This is all-out war."

"This is not my doing," said Landro. "This is your own planet turning on you."

"That's ridiculous! Planets don't have feelings or consciousness. You have shown us what your weapons can do, and this is your doing. You need to let me go back down there and let me lead our response."

"I am not letting either of you go anywhere until we start having sensible discussions. Actually, if anything triggered the Earth's response it may have been the Russians' use of scalar energy which sent its waves through the planet. But I, even I, do not have the technology to measure that."

"Actually, we do, and you are right, Commander," said the computer. "The waves set off various chain reactions, and it is likely that there will be more."

Landro and Steve looked at the computer in surprise. Landro's response was as much because the computer had spoken in English as for any other reason; Steve was simply shocked.

"So it's your fault, is it, Yuri?" said Steve, turning on the Russian, who was now breathing heavily and had paled.

"I doubt it," said Landro. "That just helped the planet achieve what it wanted to do, anyway."

Landro paused a moment, then looked directly at the two men. "Can you now see why the council has such distrust of you all? Do you think that using your plasma cannon or your lasers would have been without consequences? You cannot be let loose on the galaxy. Why is it so difficult for you to understand what is going on?" Without waiting for an answer, he turned and walked away.

The presidents were escorted, under protest, back to their separate quarters.

Landro entered the room again and asked the computer for an update on Polly's whereabouts. The computer told him that she had just arrived back in London.

He sent a text to Polly saying he would ring her in thirty minutes.

In the meantime, at the Russian air force base just outside Moscow, there was astonishment as the presidential plane was lowered silently via the tractor beam down on to the Tarmac, and a very shaken crew and entourage came down the steps.

Chapter 18

Polly had arrived back in London at 6am and gone straight to 10 Downing Street. She had scheduled a COBRA meeting for 10.00. Her phone pinged, signalling a text from Landro. She was already in the flat. On reading his message, her gut reaction was to talk to him. Then she thought that if he really was the enemy now, she shouldn't really be talking to him in private. She rang Bryony, her private secretary, and asked her to join her. She felt she needed a witness and she also thought it would be wise to record the call. Bryony had just arrived when the phone rang.

Polly could barely say 'hello'.

"Are you alone?" asked Landro.

"No, and I cannot talk to you alone now. The view of many is that you are the enemy and I probably shouldn't talk to you at all."

"Do you think that I am the enemy?"

"Did you cause the earthquakes?"

"No, of course not," said Landro. "I warned you that the planet might take things into its own hands, and that is exactly what is happening. It has used some of the effects of the Russian scalar weapons to enhance the impact but they were not the cause. The concern is that there will probably be more to come: volcanoes, earthquakes, earth slips. I asked our computer to profile the list of possibilities, and the list is long. The range and scale of these disasters is so great that it is difficult to prepare people for them."

"Will any affect the UK?"

"Of course," said Landro. "Everywhere could be affected and the planet is unlikely to divide the world into good and bad as it takes action. In its view, mankind as a whole is culpable. It is the same thing that happened with the Wei when they started fighting each other. The Earth's response to that was to trigger the great tsunamis that you know as the Great Flood."

"Can you help us prevent them, or help us with the consequences?"

"Maybe. But you know, Polly, maybe this will be the self-correcting action that the planet needs: fewer people, more understanding that the planet is not passive and that you need to work with it, not against it."

"Landro, how can you say that? That is terrible. You talked once of common humanity – what has happened to that? Not everyone is like Steve McIerney, or the Russian or Chinese presidents. Okay, a lot are but a lot aren't. I think after what happened at the UN, I could get some consensus on what we might do."

Landro was silent for a while. He then spoke slowly. "I am sorry, Polly. It may be too late for that now. Once planets decide to act, it is difficult to stop them."

"Landro, please try, and… Landro, you are human. Or are you? Maybe you are a shape-shifter or whatever it is that my sons talk about. We know nothing about you or Vendra."

To her great embarrassment and irritation she found herself crying in frustration and unable to continue for a moment.

"If what you say is true…" she continued, "your people were rescued and helped to start afresh. If you have the means then please help us, and soon, before these disasters become too much for us. As it is, the world is already reeling under the latest catastrophes."

There was a pause before he replied. "Polly, I'll see what I can do. Let me look at all the possibilities. I also need to talk to the council." And with that, he said his farewells and rang off.

Polly turned to Bryony. "Can you get me the French president? I need to speak to her before the COBRA meeting."

Five minutes later, Aurelie was on the line. "I have only a few minutes, Polly, before I meet with my security chiefs."

Polly described her conversation with Landro, sent Aurelie a copy of the recording and expressed her concerns about having any calls with Landro at all. Aurelie reassured her about the importance of keeping the lines open but also of the common sense of making recordings.

"Let me listen to the recording and I will call you later."

Polly went through to her COBRA meeting. She played the recording of the telephone conversation, and then asked what parts of the United Kingdom might be more vulnerable. For the most part, neither ministers nor military present could think of obvious examples. Then her minister for Space, David Lethbridge, spoke up. Polly had a lot of time for him. While a good politician, he was also in her view bright and intelligent, not a characteristic shared by all her political colleagues.

"I think the reference to the Great Flood is interesting.

We have already seen the dreadful impact of tsunamis on Japan, and while we are not a known earthquake zone, we would be in reach of tsunamis from areas that are. Don't forget that things other than earthquakes can cause tsunamis. A huge chunk of a Greenland glacier moving into the sea or, perhaps more likely, the volcano in the Canary Islands erupting again and triggering the collapse of one side of its cone. We know that shifted four feet or so a few years back – I remember reading an interesting piece about the risks of that in some study when I was minister for science. As I recall, it would create something called a mega-tsunami which would send waves up to 300 feet high out to hit the west coast of Africa, the Caribbean and the US eastern seaboard. The waves would not be as high here but they could still cause considerable damage. There were strong differences of view among the academic community, but still, it is the type of risk we should look at more closely."

Both scenarios were discussed and it was agreed that they should be urgently researched further. In the meantime local authorities on the coast were to be urged to look at their sea defences and the impact waves of up to 100 feet would have on them. They also agreed that Polly should make sure the UN were aware of her conversation with Landro and the subsequent discussions held at this meeting. A message was sent to the British ambassador to the UN for this to be done as soon as possible.

Chapter 19

The British ambassador briefed the assembly about the call between Polly and Landro, which elicited a mixture of reactions. The United States and Russia condemned any contact with the enemy, as they now described Landro, and deemed the conversation inappropriate. Once again, Polly's loyalties were called into question. Any future exchanges with Landro should involve only the United States and Russia as the principal players. This caused uproar from several other states, not least France, whose ambassador intervened strongly in support of the United Kingdom. She stressed that all channels available must be used and if Landro and Polly were able to talk to each other informally, then that should be encouraged. Formal negotiations were a different matter and she suggested that in the first instance the permanent members of the Security Council should provide the negotiating team, should there, of course, be anything to negotiate.

The discussion moved on to examine how to manage the current 'natural disasters' and how to prepare for any future catastrophes. The United States had managed to provide most of the support needed for the Californian disaster…although the reality was that the swallowing up of San Francisco and the areas to the north and south of it had been so total that there were depressingly few survivors.

Earthquake damage inland had been substantial and the infrastructure heavily impacted – most Interstate highways had been damaged in one way or another. But the Federal Emergency Management Agency was coping, and help had come from all over the United States. They had been able to provide help to Mexico, which had also been hit, although not as hard.

In Japan, the authorities were under huge pressure but were coping. Their main concern was again their nuclear reactors and although they were better protected than at the time of Fukushima and all the shutdown mechanisms had operated this time, there was still concern about the water damage in the longer term.

Each country agreed to look at its own risk areas for future catastrophes and to pool that information. The impact of glaciers breaking off or the collapse of the Canary Island volcano were seen as threats that needed more attention.

Up on *Touching the Heavens*, Landro and Vendra were having their own discussion. She had heard his conversation with Polly, as had Tzok.

"Is there anything we can do to prevent or mitigate future disasters? And would we want to?" asked Landro.

"If we can, maybe we should, as it would show that we hadn't caused them. At the moment, your original warning and message are lost in the anger and belief that somehow, we triggered these catastrophes," said Vendra.

She turned to Tzok and asked him. "Could we intervene?"

"Not if it is an earthquake or a volcano. We can't prevent those. And there is not a lot that we can do to mitigate the consequences. In the case of a volcano we could help clear the ash if the volume thrown into the air was so great that it risked creating a permanent winter effect for several years." Tzok shook his head.

"The most likely risk at the moment is actually the volcano in the Canaries and the risk of a landslip. I am picking up increased activity there now," added the computer.

"Actually, I do have a thought about that," said Vendra.

In the White House, Tom Peterson had his advisers around him. The ambassador to the UN had reported back on the UK findings and on the subsequent debate.

"How come the prime minister didn't call us first?" asked the acting president. "I thought we had this special relationship."

"I guess we lost that with the Moon base and agreeing the attack on Landro," replied the National Security Adviser. "It would be worth trying to rebuild that contact, Mr President, if I may suggest. We understand that she is building a closer relationship with France, and we need to make sure that we know what is going on there. Our own relationship with the government of Madame Malmaison is not that warm."

"I agree. Now what about these risks? Can you bring in the volcano, glacier and geography guys to talk about the risk of landslips et cetera?"

Three professors joined the meeting. All agreed the risks were real. In the case of glaciers collapsing into the oceans, they thought they would have enough warning to react and evacuate people. However, evacuation plans needed to be reviewed and reactivated, and that message would be sent out to each of the Atlantic coastline states. The Pacific coastline states were already in a state of emergency.

On the question of the La Palma volcano, the professor simply dismissed the threat. He remembered when this was first discussed many years previously, and the feeling at the time was that there just was not enough evidence to support the idea of an explosion of such magnitude that it would split the island and create a mega-tsunami. In the unlikely event that it did, any waves that reached the United States would be small, and there would be sufficient time to trigger any evacuation.

The acting president was about to dismiss the three professors when an aide came in and gave them a report from NASA. A satellite in the east Atlantic was picking up a huge volcanic explosion at La Palma which had split the island in half and thrown the whole western side of the island into the ocean. NASA had a satellite with live feed in the area, and this was immediately channelled through to the meeting room.

NASA were on the line at the same time. "We cannot see clearly through the ash and debris, but we can see a tsunami radiating out in all directions. It will hit West Africa very soon and then it will race across the Atlantic, hitting the Caribbean, South America and us in a few hours. We have another satellite in the area which should give us the size of the waves shortly. It is coming through now. The wave heading westwards is…" The voice fell silent for a moment. "It says here, Mr President, that the wave is 300 feet high. I will check that and come back to you."

The acting president turned to the professors. The professor who a moment ago had claimed there was little risk was now white and shaking.

"A tsunami with a 300-foot wave is just not possible…" he began.

"Well, I guess Noah probably had that same thought!"

yelled the acting president. "Get whatever warnings out that you can, NOW!"

"And we need to get you out of here as well, sir," said the National Security Adviser.

Other countries were picking up the news, and people were already starting to flee in panic. Huge traffic jams were already building up.

On the coast of Guinea a crowd had gathered on the beach. They watched in silence as the huge wall of water thundered towards the shore. The only voices were those of the preachers and priests, shouting their prayers and exhortations. They started to hear the noise of the water – a deep rumble. The air shimmered. As people braced themselves, the water seemed to hit an invisible barrier. The people on the beach gasped as the waves flew up hundreds of feet before falling back into a surging, boiling ocean. After twenty minutes the sea had returned to its normal level.

The US media did not pick up on what had happened along the African coast, and were focusing wholly on the evacuation efforts. Looting had started in some cities, and the National Guard was out in force.

But the waves never arrived – neither there, nor the Caribbean nor South America. In all cases they ran into an invisible barrier that threw the waves high into the air and back on to themselves. Gradually the barrier forced the foaming, boiling ocean back towards the Canary Islands and it was those islands that were devastated by the tsunamis. Beyond that, other than ships caught in the early surges, there were no casualties.

On *Touching the Heavens*, Landro looked at Vendra. "That," he said, "was brilliant."

The two captured presidents had been brought to the

bridge and had watched the whole event unfold, incredulous.

"How did you do that?"

"This is a research vessel but we also have equipment that we use when terraforming planets. We are able to put force fields around the terraforming activities to contain them. It struck me that if we deployed the shields we use for that around the island when it exploded, it might work. We had to focus on West Africa first, which is why it took longer to get the other shield projectors into place. But it worked," said Vendra, with a small smile.

"It sure did," said Steve, "but why did you bother if you want us humans destroyed?"

"We don't want you destroyed," said Landro. "We want you to stop destroying yourselves. You have antagonised your planet to the point where it is now fighting back. Doesn't this convince you that something has to change?"

"Landro, we need to get back to our people," said the president, wearily. "I am of no use here."

"I'll return you both when you tell me what your plan is, going forward."

Chapter 20

The acting president was already aloft in Air Force One when the news of the barriers reached him. The head of the air force ran the footage from both NASA and a couple of military satellites.

"This is really interesting, Mr President. It may be the first picture we have of the Sirian ship."

The satellite feed showed the huge vessel uncloaked, and tiny vessels being dispersed initially in the direction of the West African coast and then out to the west, north and south of La Palma. The satellite also caught the shimmer of the power shields.

"I wonder if the demand for power was such that the ship couldn't keep up its cloaking shields as well. It's a hell of a size and proves that the view of the Tall Whites was correct when they said *Sumer* wasn't the main vessel. We've got our analysts examining this footage closely at the moment. It may show a vulnerability in the main vessel that it does not have limitless power sources," reported the general.

"Thanks, Jimmy. Thinking of the Tall Whites, what has happened to them? I was never as much in the loop as Steve was. Are they still at Nellis?"

"Well, most, possibly all, have been leaving. I think they were shocked by the attack on the plasma cannon facilities on the Moon base but they also recognised that their vessel had not been attacked. They have agreed to leave the vessel there so we are not evacuating it. We have also picked up more communications than usual back to their home world, however, we are unable to decrypt them."

As they watched the satellite feeds, a sudden bright flash illuminated the still-uncloaked Sirian vessel. The vessel began to move away at high speed, with more flashes following in its wake. A shaft of light from the Sirian ship caused a small explosion, then the appearance of another smaller vessel which had itself been cloaked, and finally a much bigger explosion.

"What the hell was that?" shouted the acting president. "Who's attacking them?"

On *Touching the Heavens*, Landro was asking the same question. He had been very conscious that in order to power the shields to their maximum, they had had to de-cloak, which meant they would inevitably be visible to satellites. But it struck him that this could be an advantage, as their role in deflecting the tsunamis would be very clear for all to see.

In order to speed up the recharging of the power sources, the computer had left the vessel uncloaked as it moved back into near-Earth orbit. It had, however, picked up the arrival of another vessel relatively close by and was able to raise its protective shields, just in time as an energy blast hit *Touching the Heavens* close to the bridge.

The huge ship rocked under the blast. The computer recognised that their power sources could not survive too many blasts and started to move the vessel away at some speed, but not before firing one of its remote mining scalar energy drills towards the unknown craft. To the surprise of everyone on board, this penetrated the shields of the other vessel, causing a minor explosion. As a result, the cloaking device failed and a ripple of flame ran along the whole vessel, which then exploded in a shower of debris. The force of the explosion of the subspace drives shook *Touching the Heavens* for a second time.

"Computer!" called Landro, "Did you identify the vessel?"

"It was an Arisi design, but not a vessel we have seen before. It was surprisingly lightly armed and protected. I think they must have felt that the depletion of our own shields when we diverted power to the shield array against the tsunamis would have weakened us enough for them to break through. It was closer to success than I would have liked."

"The Arisi, or Tall Whites as you call them, are your allies, Mr McIerney. Was this your doing?"

The president simply stared, ashen-faced. "Not to my knowledge, Landro. Until you arrived, we had never discussed other races with them. They had asked for a base on Earth and on the Moon in return for sharing some technology with us. They had helped us establish the Moon base and provided the transport for that in the early stages. The US now has its own vessels that can reach the base. They had also promised us that at some stage we could send a delegation to their home world, and we were preparing for that. We asked them about you when you first arrived and it was clear that they did not think you were here on a friendly mission and that their own previous contacts with the galactic council had been hostile."

"Did you ask them for help against us?"

The president looked uncomfortable. "Well, not in so

many words, and we did not have the impression that they would help. The report back had suggested that they would rather stay below the radar."

"They clearly changed their minds!"

"Did you know about this?" said Landro to President Andrinov.

"Certainly not the attack, and until recently we knew very little about the contact the US had with these aliens."

At the word 'aliens', Tzok gave him a long quizzical look and then turned back to the computer.

Vendra spoke up. "I suspect they know that they now have no future on Earth, and that their plans for using humans is at the very least on hold, so they thought they would try to destroy this ship as a parting shot – a literal parting shot."

"What do you mean, 'using humans'?" asked the president.

"The very reason we want to stop you leaving the planet is a reason for the Arisi to use you – as expendable storm troopers for their own ambitions. There are plenty of areas of space where the council's influence is limited or non-existent and this is where the Arisi and others like them thrive. That's what brought them here. They may not have appreciated how long we had been observing you for and thought that they were safe here."

The computer interjected. "There may be other Arisi ships around here. We need to retreat to a safer location where I can make a thorough check."

With that, the space around *Touching the Heavens* shimmered, and the ship disappeared.

Chapter 21

Aboard Air Force One, the acting president and his team were discussing what they had just seen.

The head of the air force was the first to speak. "If that is just a research vessel, I would hate to see what their battleships are like. We are analysing the footage now. With the disappearance of both ships, we have sent two of our X-47Bs to the site to sift through the debris and see what we can learn. There may even be survivors from the second ship…although given the force of the explosion it is difficult to see how."

An aide entered. "I have the UK prime minister on the line for you, Mr President."

"Tom, Polly here. I am sure you have better coverage than we do. What has been going on? Were you responsible for that attack on Landro's ship?"

"Polly, nice to hear from you too. I'll check what coverage we have that we can share. As for the attack, we have no idea. Your buddy Landro packs quite a punch, doesn't he? And he also seems to have picked up on your plea about common humanity with his intervention on the tsunamis. Have you spoken to him again recently?"

"Not since the call that I shared. Are you sure you or your allies at Nellis weren't behind that attack?"

"Polly, what's at Nellis is not what you think," said the acting president, realising that he sounded as unconvincing as he felt.

"Tom, at some point you need to come clean and share what you have been up to. We need to face this crisis as a united planet. Anyway, I would appreciate it if you would share as much as you can." Polly ended the call.

"Self-righteous Brits," muttered the general under his breath.

Another aide entered. "I have the president on the line."

"Whose president?" asked Tom.

"Our president," said the aide sharply and handed him the phone.

"My God, Steve, where are you? How are you?"

"I am on Landro's ship. I'm here with Yuri. We are both okay although Landro refuses to let us go. That attack was by the Tall Whites. Landro and his buddies call them the Arisi. They reckon it was a parting shot. You had better check what is happening at Nellis. Anyway, I am fine, if pissed off with being stuck up here and having fruitless exchanges with Landro, Vendra and Tzok. Yuri and I are trying to persuade Landro to send us back but he keeps saying he will only do so when we commit to supporting his mission to Earth. Anyway, for the time being, he has moved his vessel to—"

The line went dead.

"Sorry, Mr President, I can't let you disclose our location," said the computer.

Back in the United Kingdom, Polly was attending another COBRA meeting. She was reporting back on the exchange with the US acting president, when an aide entered the room and passed her a message.

Polly read aloud: "Apparently Steve McIerney has been in touch with his VP, who reports that he and Yuri Andrinov are still aboard Landro's ship – presumably the large one."

The meeting continued for another half hour but the sense that things were out of control was palpable, and Polly could not help feeling depressed as she returned to Number 10.

After a moment's reflection, she called in Bryony and said she was going to try to ring Landro. She had little expectation of success and was taken aback when he answered.

"Landro, what is going on? Who attacked you? What happened?"

Landro explained about the Arisi. "We are okay although we are checking the ship and it may be that we need to return to Qrxa."

"Will you take Steve and Yuri with you?"

"I am not sure." There was a moment's silence before Landro continued. "I think maybe I should return to London so that you and I can meet. I have been thinking about your comments that maybe Vendra and I are not human. I was actually very shocked by that and the idea that I might be a shape-shifter or some such. I could give another interview and broadcast. I am concerned that attitudes are polarising and we are being seen as the enemy. If I came to London, perhaps that would help shape a more constructive response. You might want to invite your French colleague over as well."

Polly replied in as measured a way as she could, agreeing that this was an excellent idea and that she looked forward to welcoming him again.

Landro promised to confirm his plans once they were clear about the state of their ship, and ended the call.

Polly had tried to sound matter-of-fact about Landro's proposal but she was surprised by how her heart was thumping as she turned to Bryony.

Bryony Mitchell had been head of her private office for over two years and they got on well. They were similar ages and both had two children. Although Polly had not said anything to her, Bryony could see that Polly found Landro attractive, and on balance she thought that this was a good thing. Although she didn't know about the discussion with the French president in detail, she shared the view that there needed to be a constructive dialogue with Landro, Vendra and the others, and so far the Russians, Americans and Chinese were failing miserably.

"Prime Minister, this may seem a strange idea given everything that is going on, but if Landro does come back to London, why don't you invite him to spend more time here and get a feel for the way we live. At the moment his knowledge is all theoretical – what he has studied and had implanted. You and he clearly have a good rapport," Polly felt herself reddening at that comment but Bryony ignored it, "and it must be worth building on that. You are in a good position to build on the hard work you had done before the debacle at the UN and show him that there is more to Earth than what he has experienced so far."

Polly looked at her a moment and then laughed. "Are you suggesting that I ask him on a date?"

Bryony laughed back. "You could do a lot worse, Prime Minister!"

Chapter 22

The visit was arranged for two days later. The process of the first three visits was repeated. *Sumer* descended silently over Hyde Park and the small capsule holding Landro and Vendra descended. To everyone's surprise, the US and Russian presidents also appeared. Polly and her support team, along with Aurelie Malmaison and her team, were waiting to greet them. The press and media were in full attendance, and beyond the security cordon a huge crowd had gathered.

"Welcome back," said Polly, holding out her hand to Landro and Vendra, who returned her warm greeting. The two presidents were rather more perfunctory and looked rather embarrassed.

They all headed for the podium, and Landro spoke at length about what had happened since the meeting at the UN. He described in detail the nature of the Russian weapon that had been deployed against *Sumer*, or at least the image of *Sumer*; how Vendra's ingenuity with the tractor beam had enabled them to create the impression of success while ensuring their own survival; he talked about the American presence on the Moon, the plasma cannon that they had developed there; he told the story of the Arisi, their presence on Earth and in particular how long they had had a presence at Nellis; and he described how the planet was in many ways a living entity and that when threatened, as it was now, it would try to re-establish equilibrium by whatever climatic or geological ways that it could.

He invited questions from the floor. The first questions were aimed primarily at the US president. Why had the Americans covered up their relationship with the Arisi for so long? Why had they hidden their own technological advances which would have helped other nations, and, indeed, Americans themselves?

Steve looked very ill at ease. "I accept that when this is described in the way Commander Landro has done, it looks bad." He paused. "Very bad, I guess. If I am honest, I did not know all the details myself until recently but in talking to the two commanders and the Sirians during our enforced R&R on their ship, it became clear that the reason both they and the Arisi came here was because of the technology deployed in World War II. For the Sirians, this was a cause of concern and they have, as we now know, continued to monitor our planet. For the Arisi, it is now clear to me, this was an opportunity. The original visit was made in the context of asking for an Earth base where they could make repairs to their trading vessels and source supplies. I guess we took that at face value, and it gave us a chance to access technology that we felt would help us in the Cold War. So, no, we didn't share it. The problem is that the longer you keep a secret, as with Roswell, the harder it is to be open about it."

He paused. Polly admired Steve's frankness and honesty, although she wondered how it would be received in Washington and the Pentagon.

The next questions were aimed at Landro. Were there likely to be more earthquakes and if so could he help prevent them?

He replied that he couldn't rule it out – it was not within his control.

Suddenly there was a commotion. The US president had jumped off the small dais and was running towards the media. He suddenly stopped, almost in mid-air – his arms and legs were pumping but he wasn't moving. Gradually he moved back towards the dais. Vendra lowered the small gadget she held, with its portable tractor beam, and whispered something in his ear. He went red and sat down heavily on one of the chairs. Vendra gave him a glass of water.

There was a moment's silence.

"Are you keeping the two presidents prisoner?" shouted a reporter.

Irritated, Landro looked at Steve before answering. "They will stay with me while we discuss the challenges I laid down at the UN and how they are going to contribute to solving them." He paused. "I think it will be best if we return to the ship, and Vendra and I will return tomorrow."

The group of four made their way to the small shuttle and headed back up to *Sumer*. It accelerated away.

Over in Washington, Tom was at the White House with his team around him. In response to Steve's comments, Tom wondered if he had been drugged. He was just saying how unhelpful it had been to have said so much and how important it was to get the message to the American people right when they saw Steve's attempt to escape…and its total failure.

"Oh God, that's awful and humiliating," said the National

Security Adviser. "He looks like one of those Disney cartoon characters – arms and legs whirring but going nowhere."

"At least he tried," said the acting president. "Andrinov just stood there panting heavily. Okay, get me a text – I need to talk to the American people again tonight, if not sooner."

In London, Polly and Aurelie were at 10 Downing Street.

"So much for that plan," said Polly. "Why on earth did he bring Steve and Yuri with him?"

"To show that they were okay, alive and well," said Aurelie. "Steve was clearly very alive and well! And it helped that he is now admitting what the Americans have been up to. Perhaps we should talk to the acting president."

Polly agreed and asked Bryony to set it up. A few minutes later, Tom was on the line.

"Why didn't you Brits try to rescue Steve and the Russian, or intervene when Steve made a run for it? You could have helped," was his opening gambit.

Polly was taken aback. "You know that isn't logical, Tom. We didn't know they would be there, and anyway, we were there to have a dialogue with Landro and Vendra. As it turned out any rescue effort would have been futile. At least he was good enough to confirm what Landro had said about Nellis, the Tall Whites and your Moon base."

Tom growled, "Landro is just making this stuff up, and Steve was probably drugged."

At this point, Aurelie spoke up. "Monsieur le acting president, Aurelie Malmaison here. Surely you must see that it is now time for you to stop these games. Confirm to the world that what has been said is right, plus anything else that you have been hiding. We need everything out in the open and then we can start with a clean sheet to solve the challenges that Landro has set us. You and the Russians cannot go on with this macho posturing – it is helping no one, and certainly not your president."

"As always, a pleasure to talk to you ladies," said Tom sarcastically. "I'll be in touch." He rang off.

Aurelie shrugged and turned back to Polly. "These Americans! They are hopeless, *n'est-ce pas?*" she said. "Still we have Landro and Vendra coming back tomorrow, and we must plan. What are your ideas?"

After a long discussion, Polly sent a text to Landro with her thoughts and asked how long he could remain. She asked if he wanted her to arrange accommodation or whether he and Vendra would continue to use *Sumer*.

He texted back to confirm he would be staying for two or three days but they would use *Sumer*.

Chapter 23

The following morning the shuttle descended, but this time only Landro and Vendra emerged. As agreed by text, they started with a media conference.

Polly kicked it off. "Landro, Vendra, can you start by telling us a bit more about yourselves and about the humans on Qrxa and elsewhere in the galaxy?"

For the first time, Vendra came forward to take the lead. "Landro and I grew up in a human settlement. The Sirians made us very welcome but their culture is very different to ours and so we have tended to stick together. We are also, as you have seen, rather larger than most Sirians and so while we can travel freely around the planet, it makes sense to live in an area built to our size. Our community currently lives in an off-world construct high above Qrxa – you have seen part of it in the films we showed you earlier. Because of implants, our education is quite quick in terms of factual knowledge, so we tend to focus on problem-solving and on developing other faculties, such as intuition and mind communication. Humans and Sirians complement each other, I think, and I hope Tzok would agree with that," she said, with a smile. "Sirians are very technically and technologically minded but they do not have human instinct. We can add that. We like to think that we see solutions that neither they nor their computers can see.

"That said, there is no doubt that carrying as we do the same genetic make-up as you, we have our flaws and challenges, which the Sirians struggle to understand. They are not emotional in the way we are and they do not search out relationships in the personal way we humans do. We still get together to have children. The Sirian approach to reproduction, and, indeed, to the community, is much more technological and practical. That works well for them. Some human groups have tried to emulate it but without adaptive implants, it does not work for us.

"I have two children, much the same age as yours, Polly, a boy and a girl. And in case you have been wondering, Landro is actually my brother. He and I have worked on many missions, including ones involving other human groups. Landro?"

"As Vendra said, we grew up together. Both our parents were engineers but they still encouraged me when my strengths seemed to lie more with comparative cultures and history. And now we are here. And oh, before you ask, I do not have a partner or any children."

He looked briefly at Polly, who flushed, much to Aurelie's amusement.

They took a wide range of questions – about what Qrxa was like, what it was like living in an off-world constructed environment, about the differences between them and the Sirians to which they had referred, and about the other human settlements in the galaxy. There were also more questions about Earth's past civilisations and about the Wei.

A journalist asked, "So, are you here to help us or destroy us?"

Landro looked at him and replied, "As I have said several times to the US and Russian presidents, I am here to help you stop destroying yourselves and this planet, your home. How that happens is up to all of you."

The media conference closed and the key players, Polly, Bryony, her key defence team, Aurelie with her team, Landro and Vendra moved to a coach which took them off to 10 Downing Street.

For the evening, Polly had decided to risk a concert – Brahms, Sibelius and Beethoven. They had a box at the Royal Festival Hall. Security was very tight but there was still an audience and everyone peered up at the box before the music began.

Polly and Aurelie were intrigued by the clothes that Vendra and Landro wore. They seemed to wear the same shape of clothes every day but with different colouring. This evening they were wearing garments that seemed to change colours. There were no adornments other than the various gadgets that they seemed to wear at all times. Then Polly noticed that Vendra had attached a small blue gem stone on a setting in her silver hair, matching the one nestling among the gadgets on her waist. She asked Vendra about them, saying that it was the first time that she had seen her wearing such jewellery.

Vendra laughed. "It is rare for us to wear such things but I know women here do and so I thought I would do so as well. And I like them. I don't think human women will have changed so much over the millennia," she said, her eyes twinkling.

Aurelie leant over to Polly and whispered, "Common humanity – *c'est bon!*"

As the final chorus of Beethoven's 9th Symphony died

away and the applause rang out, Polly and Aurelie were startled to see tears rolling down the cheeks of both their guests.

Landro composed himself. "We have no such music. The Sirians do not have music, and our music has not moved on from the tribal chants and rhythms we took with us. It kept us together and has not been developed at all. Our music reminds us of who we are. This is totally different. I had never heard your music before."

They travelled back to Hyde Park in silence.

The next morning, Polly had arranged a tour of London in an open double-decker. Polly and Landro and Aurelie and Vendra sat in the front seats of the top deck. Landro had dismissed suggestions that they should not be in the open despite the misgivings of all the security personnel, who packed the seats behind them. Along the route were armed police, both at street level and on the rooftops.

"I haven't done this since I became prime minister," said Polly.

"I haven't done this since I came here on an exchange visit more years ago than I can remember," added Aurelie.

If the atmosphere behind them was tense, the travelling group of four were very relaxed. The implanted information that Vendra and Landro had taken on board was formidable so they knew what they were seeing and the history behind it all but as they said, it made a real difference to see it for real.

As they went past Buckingham Palace, the coach turned in through the gates, through the arch and up to the main entrance. Waiting on the step were the King and Queen.

"What is this?" said Landro. "I thought your king only meets heads of state, and I am far from such."

Polly laughed: "But Aurelie is a head of state, Landro, and so royal protocol is satisfied. And he is desperate to meet you both."

It was an incongruous sight, seeing the party descend from the upper deck of the bus to be greeted by the King.

"Madame le Président, a great pleasure to see you, albeit in somewhat unexpected circumstances." He turned to Polly. "Prime Minister." He nodded and she curtsied as she said, "Your Majesty," much to Landro and Vendra's bemusement. They instead shook hands and the King ushered them all indoors.

The King was fascinated to hear at first hand everything they had to say and was clearly reluctant to let them leave. He even asked if at some time, he might visit their ship. Two hours later, the party climbed into the bus for the remainder of the tour.

The mood was good and relaxed, and Polly had to explain the etiquette involving the King. Landro and Vendra remained bemused, and Aurelie just raised her eyebrows.

As they turned down Buckingham Gate, shots rang out. Everyone ducked.

"Stay down!" yelled Polly's personal security guard who was right behind her. His French counterpart almost threw himself on top of the French president.

A truck came at speed out of a side road. It was about to crash into a police car blocking the junction when it stopped in its tracks, as if it had hit a wall. Polly looked up. Vendra was standing on her seat, holding a gadget in each hand.

A small drone hovered above them. A glow descended and provided a protective envelope around them. Polly hadn't noticed it before and wondered if it had been cloaked. Her security people had said nothing. The stalled truck suddenly exploded with violent ferocity. The bus was unscathed but she could see the fragments bouncing off the shield. It was clear that the blast had caused considerable damage.

Vendra looked shaken. "I am sorry. I only had time to strengthen the shield around the bus and couldn't put a shield around the lorry itself in time."

Under police escort, the bus sped away back to Downing Street. Everyone on the bus was shocked but no one was hurt.

Aurelie and Polly convened briefly before the French president returned to the French embassy, under heavy guard.

Against all the advice of her security people, Polly announced she was going back to the scene of the explosion.

"It is too dangerous," said her security chief, "and we do not know if the gunmen are still there."

"I am not going to hide away," replied Polly. "We must not be intimidated by this."

"I cannot permit it," said the security chief.

"You will not stop me," said Polly.

Vendra stepped forward. "I will come with you. I can protect you."

"So can we," said the security chief rather testily, "but it is still very unwise."

Vendra looked at him. "I know you can, but the fact is we can provide a protective shield just as we did with the bus."

The group set off in three vehicles, under police escort, and soon arrived at the scene. It was chaotic. The shield had protected the bus but the blast had only partially been absorbed by it and there had been a ricochet effect that had added to the damage to the buildings and passers-by. The emergency services were everywhere, dealing with the injured and removing the dead.

Polly was stunned. Noticing a bloodstained mother with her child she went over to them. The woman was in shock. The medic with them let the prime minister through. Polly only had time to say, "I am so sorry" and to squeeze the woman's hand before the nurse asked her to move on.

"I am sorry, Prime Minister, but we need to treat these people urgently. These are the most lightly injured. The serious casualties have all been taken to St Thomas'."

Landro and Vendra had been standing behind the prime minister. Vendra came forward and, looking at the child who had a long gash in her leg, she produced another gadget from her tunic and before the medic could object, she ran it along the gash very slowly. To everyone's astonishment, the gash disappeared.

"Perhaps I can help at the hospital," said Vendra.

On the way, Vendra explained how the Sirian technology worked, how it accelerated healing.

They were met by the head of the hospital who had been warned about the arrival of the prime minister.

"Prime Minister, I understand your wish to visit and to be seen here but this really is not a good time. We have twenty people here who are seriously injured."

Polly ignored his rather patronising tone. "We are actually here to help, Professor. It turns out that the Sirians have capabilities in medicine way beyond ours, and Vendra here is happy to look at the injured."

"I cannot allow that. With the greatest respect, it would be totally unprofessional and illegal to allow anyone else to deal with our patients." He was about to continue when he seemed to freeze.

"Professor?" said Polly. She noticed Landro staring at the professor, a look of deep concentration on his face.

"Landro, what are you doing? Whatever it is, stop!"

"He is fine but talking here does not help the patients. I suggest we proceed."

He and Vendra exchanged a quick look and then entered the hospital, followed by Polly and her team. The hospital security seemed unable to decide what to do and in the end did nothing. Vendra asked which floor the injured were on, and they all headed up in the lift to the ward and operating areas.

Vendra did not go into the operating theatre but round the wards.

Polly and the doctors watched in amazement as she used her gadgets. At one point she said something to Landro who disappeared to the roof and came back with more gadgets, which had arrived via a drone that he had summoned from *Sumer*. After four hours, all the patients were stabilised and the wounds of most were healed. Vendra was unable to do anything at that time for a man who had lost an eye and a woman who had lost her lower leg, but otherwise deeps gashes and intestinal injuries seemed to magically disappear. She promised to come back and help with the limb and eye regrowth.

As she had gone round the beds, the surgeons and doctors following her had watched initially with scepticism and then with awe. This included the professor who had greeted them earlier. He could recall his conversation with them but could not work out how it was that he had been left there while they entered the hospital.

When Vendra had finished, her costume was smeared with blood and she was exhausted. "I need to go back to *Sumer*, Landro." She turned to Polly and to Polly's surprise, hugged her.

Landro and Vendra went up to the roof where the shuttle had arrived and headed back to their spacecraft.

Polly was faced with a crowd of reporters as she left the front entrance and tried to explain, as best as she could, what had happened.

Chapter 24

The newspaper headlines the next morning read 'Miracle Worker', featuring stories from the doctors at St Thomas' and pictures of the healing of the child's gash at the site of the explosion and a blood-spattered Vendra alongside Landro as they stepped into their shuttle. One headline included a picture of Vendra, with the caption 'The Sirian Saint'.

Reports covered the explosion itself. A fundamentalist group had claimed responsibility, saying that the Sirians were agents of evil and had to be destroyed. The police had tracked the lorry to a rental firm in East London and were busy rounding up suspects. The gunman had not yet been caught.

Landro and Vendra were now back on the main vessel, talking to the two presidents, who had been watching everything unfold on screens in the lounge area where they spent most of their day.

"Those gadgets you used in the hospital, would you share those with us?" asked the Russian president.

Vendra paused and then said, "The problem is that like all technology, this can be used for both peaceful and military purposes. It is clear that this planet is unable to function peacefully. This latest attack just reinforced to all of us how big our…and your…challenge is to get things back on track. You have spent a lot of time together and with Tzok – do you have any ideas yet?"

Steve replied, "This is the longest period of enforced rest I have had for a long time, and yet strangely, it has been useful to discuss our issues with Yuri here, another world leader, without the risk of being interrupted by yet another crisis. It has also been interesting to talk to Tzok and the other Sirian who spends time with us, Trng. They have described not only Qrxa but also planets in other galaxies. We have seen so much footage of these other places. We have also seen the consequences of war using the weapons that we both and the Chinese have been developing. We have seen examples of planets taking things into their own hands as is happening here. I had thought that was nonsense but we now both accept that it can happen." Yuri nodded in agreement. "But if we understand the issues and the bigger picture better, I really am not sure how to make the changes. We cannot accept randomly reducing our population, and as you have said so often, violence is a part of our character…as you saw so vividly yesterday. But I can see now that somehow we need to drive the changes you describe, Landro."

Steve fell silent and looked rather reflectively out of the long picture window towards the small ball that was the Earth.

Landro and Vendra left and returned to the bridge.

"I think we should return the presidents," said Landro. "They have come a long way in their thinking and maybe they can now start to influence the debate. We should also start to stream these videos of other worlds that Trng has been showing them."

"I agree. They have certainly changed their attitude."

Landro rang Polly and told her what was being planned. He also arranged for the two presidents to speak to their respective offices. They would return to London at 10.00 the next morning.

The next day, at exactly 10am, the ritual that had now unfolded several times, did so once again. At 9.45 Polly left 10 Downing Street for Hyde Park. The crowds were large as reports of the release of the two presidents had been on the news. At 9.58 the small craft detached itself from *Sumer* and dropped down at Hyde Park, where a permanent marquee had been set up.

Polly waited, along with her staff. Beside her were the US and Russian ambassadors and their staff. It had been agreed that there would be no press conference, and the cameras were to be kept at a distance. Landro and Vendra stepped out of the shuttle, followed by the two presidents. The Sirians shook hands with each of them and they each stepped towards their respective ambassadors. The Russian ambassador embraced his president, shook his hand warmly, and both men spoke briefly to Polly before departing. The US president was slower to move – perhaps remembering the painful experience of his last visit to Hyde Park. He and the ambassador shook hands briefly and he made to go over to Polly. The ambassador had an urgent word in his ear and Steve nodded.

"Prime Minister," he said, "if you helped in my release, my thanks. There is much I would like to discuss with you but the ambassador and others are anxious for me to leave. I will be in touch."

He shook hands with Polly and was whisked away in a convoy of cars towards the embassy, south of the river.

Landro turned to Polly. "May I talk to your media?"

Polly was slightly taken aback but said, "Of course."

Inwardly she laughed at his courtesy since he was perfectly capable of taking over all the TV channels for direct transmission without her permission. The media who had been kept at a distance were now invited to come forward.

Landro began. "I hope that Vendra and I have demonstrated enough that our mission here is not hostile. Our objective is not to destroy the Earth – although I hear many voices saying that is why we are here – but to prevent you destroying yourselves, or the Earth itself turning on you. You have already witnessed the power of your much-abused planet and I fear there may be more such events.

"Our intention now is to start broadcasting through your TV stations and streaming through other outlets information and films about your galaxy – about the species that inhabit it, about the Grand Council, the great events that have shaped it, including extinction events where species have destroyed themselves or their planet has turned on them.

"We want you to see what you are part of so that you can encourage your politicians to make the changes that are required, the changes that I laid out before the UN a few weeks ago."

With that, he stopped and turned to Polly. She had not been expecting his speech and therefore was not as prepared as she liked to be when addressing the media.

"Commander, it can only help for us to learn more about the galaxy of which we are a part and about which we have known so little. You talk about influencing politicians. The challenge you have given us is daunting but I am confident that we can meet it," she said, hoping that her lack of confidence in that point didn't come through. "I am continuing to work

123

with my colleagues at the UN to develop the plans."

Polly paused before resuming. "On a more personal note, I would like to record publicly my thanks to you both for your help in containing the effects of the Canary Islands tsunami and yesterday after the attack. Your sense of common humanity shone through and all of us will remember the compassion you showed.

"As for the attack itself, the police have several suspects in custody and are continuing their searches. These attacks are always shocking and it is a challenge to our society that there are those who continue to believe that violence is the way to change things and to be heard. You, our visitors from Sirius, have shone a bright light on this aspect of our nature and to be blunt, have said explicitly that without change we may destroy ourselves and at the very least we will not be allowed to leave this planet. These are profound challenges. I cannot pretend to have the answers but across our societies we must more than ever address them if we are ever to take our place on the wider stage that you have described and shown to us. I am happy to take questions."

After half an hour the Q&A came to an end and Landro, Vendra and Polly headed out of the marquee.

"I would like to return to the hospital," said Vendra. "I have brought more equipment with me."

"Of course," said Polly, and they made their way to the PM's car and security escorts.

In the White House, the acting president stared scornfully at the TV.

"She really has bought all this crap that Landro has been coming out with. We need to be really careful with her. God knows whose side she is on now."

An assistant came in to say that the president was at the embassy in London and was ready for a videoconference. The connection was put through.

"Hi Steve, it's good to see you. Are you okay? What did those guys do to you and Andrinov? And have you been watching all this stuff that the Brits have been spouting? Polly really is in the pockets of the Sirians!"

"Hi Tom, good to see you too. I am fine. I was well looked after, and Yuri and I had some useful conversations, as I did with Landro, Vendra and the Sirian guys that were with them. Things look a lot different from 180 miles up, I can tell you. I don't think Polly is as misguided as we might have thought. I've learnt and seen a lot, which I will share with you all when I am back in the White House. Juan here tells me that there is a plane waiting for me so I am going to head off shortly."

"Sounds good. But just to be clear, Steve, we need you to go for a full check-up before you return. You know the protocol for returning astronauts, and I guess they apply to you now. We also need to check that those aliens haven't messed with your head. So you'll be taken straight to our special facilities when you land."

"C'mon, Tom, this is a different situation. People need to see that their president is back, and I need to talk to the nation to tell them what happened to me and to reassure them."

"I'm sorry, Steve, everyone here agrees that it has to be this way. Let's get you back and checked out and then you'll be back in the White House. Sorry, I've got to go. It's been an early start here and it is only going to get busier."

Steve was shocked. He looked at the ambassador. "Did you know about this?"

"Yes, I did. We all agree that it is best. You need to be checked out. I know you feel fine but who knows what really happened to you up there?"

"Can I go out for some fresh air first?"

"I'm afraid not," said the ambassador, embarrassed. "My instructions are to take you straight to the airport and on to the plane."

With that, two embassy staff and a couple of guards entered the room and guided the president to a waiting vehicle.

Back at the hospital, the staff rushed out to greet Vendra. This time the head of the hospital welcomed her and led her quickly through to the wards where the injured were being treated. Having checked on the cases she had focused on the previous day, Vendra went to see the man who had lost an eye. She took a device out of her pocket, analysed his good eye and took a blood sample from his left arm. She turned to the man.

"I will return with a new eye and help insert it. You will be fine."

She went over to the woman who had lost her lower limb. This time she produced a different device. She asked for the bandages to be removed from the damaged leg. The nurses started to protest but the head of the hospital nodded his agreement. Vendra used one of her devices to spin a semi-transparent shape of a leg on the bloody stump. She then injected something into the leg just above the wound. She turned to the doctors who were watching.

"I have stimulated the limb to regrow. It should be quick – about a month." She gave a pack of syringes to the nurses. "You need to inject one of these daily, at the same time as the injection I just made. If there are any problems you can reach me on this device." She handed over a small device that looked like a smartphone. "I have configured it like one of your smartphones," she explained, "but there is only one number: mine. I'm afraid you cannot add other numbers. Please don't try to deconstruct it – it is single moulding and cannot be opened. I would also suggest that you don't try scanning it either," she added.

With that, Vendra rejoined Landro and Polly who, with Bryony and other staff, had been watching from a distance. They all left the hospital for 10 Downing Street.

They headed into a small conference room where Polly, her senior security ministers and several advisers were present.

Polly made the introductions and explained that she wanted to explore with Landro and Vendra what was to happen next. She also indicated that she was keen to discuss with them how they might be able to help with the targets they had set everyone.

Addressing Landro, she admitted, "It is no secret that I am struggling to get any real changes agreed with the other countries at the UN, as you know, and it strikes me that you or others on the council will have dealt with similar situations in the past."

"We have had some thoughts," replied Landro, "but I need to talk to Vrin and the council. The difficulty I have is that despite the very clear message I gave to the leaders of the planet, the response has largely been disappointing. I know you believe us and are trying your best. But the attacks on me at the UN, the consistent concealing of the truth about contacts with other non-Earth species, and even, I regret to say, the lorry attack on us here all simply reinforce the fears of the council. I had hoped that the discussions Tzok and Trng had with the US and Russian presidents would have convinced them of the need to act urgently. In fact it did at the time, but I am concerned that the US president seems to have disappeared from public view and, if the call we intercepted is right, is being held at a secure facility and prevented from seeing his family. Andrinov has not made any public announcement yet, although he may be waiting until he is back in Moscow."

"I will ring Tom after the meeting and ask about Steve," said Polly.

"We may be gone for a few days. We need to report back to the council and bring them fully up to speed on what has been happening here."

They said their farewells and Landro and Vendra headed back to the shuttle. Polly caught Landro's eye as he left, and she realised that she was disappointed she wouldn't be seeing or hearing from him for a few days.

Chapter 25

Vendra and Landro said little as the small shuttle rejoined *Sumer*, which in turn rejoined the bigger ship. There was much for them to reflect on.

They sat with Tzok, Trng and the other Sirians to talk through the options.

"We knew that this would not be straightforward," said Tzok. "These situations never are. I also wonder if it was a mistake to send two humans to talk to the humans here on this planet."

Before Landro could reply, Vendra spoke up. "I always appreciate your directness, Tzok, and your view may turn out to be correct. However, for the moment, I genuinely believe it is worth persevering. You certainly convinced the US and Russian presidents of the need to act now, Landro has established a genuinely warm relationship with the UK prime minister and it is clear that the French president supports her. On the other hand, we have monitored the conversations in various other countries and it is clear that opinions vary hugely. Can I suggest a way forward? I propose that we return to Qrxa to brief Vrin and the council, explore some thoughts that Landro and I have had with you now, and subject to what the council says, return to brief the Earth's leaders at the UN again."

Tzok was silent for a moment and then turned to Landro and asked him to share his thoughts.

Landro began. "As you say, this is not the first time we have found ourselves in this situation. It would not in our view be a desirable outcome to destroy the humans on this planet. Vendra and I recognise that the hybridisation of humans makes this different in certain ways, but the civilisation here has a richness as well as a violent side. I would also stress that humans like Vendra and I are no more a problem on the worlds where they have settled than any other species. The problem here is that humans have had no real competition to keep their worst behaviours in check. In the rest of the galaxy there are many sentient and more advanced species who would and could prevent humans running riot."

Tzok said, "When I arrived here, I thought the decisions would be easy. However, I found the two presidents more intelligent and their ideas more constructive than I had expected. Despite their public statements, once they were exposed privately to the reality of the Earth's situation, they showed the ability to flex their thoughts. And so, I think you may be right that humans, or should I say, these humans," he glanced at Vendra and Landro with what passed for a smile, "may be assisted in time to become constructive members of the galaxy. But it is still clear to me that humans must not be allowed to have the technology for interstellar flight, and we must prevent races like the Arisi trying to use humans for their own purposes. So, what would your proposals be?"

They discussed various ideas and then decided they

were ready to go back to Qrxa. The computer took over and as with the original outward journey, they found themselves emerging in what seemed an extraordinarily short period close to Qrxa. The ship navigated to its docking port above the off-world facility, and Landro, Vendra and Tzok took a shuttle down to the off-world facility itself and then on via the space elevator to the surface of the planet. The remaining crew were responsible for checking the ship for any damage following the Arisi attack, and to resupply. It was taken for granted that they would be returning to Earth.

The trio had to wait two days for the opportunity to meet Vrin and used the time to network and talk to other senior leaders to test and refine their ideas.

At the meeting, Vrin listened as they described recent events. He had read the reports that had been sent through but he found it valuable to have the full picture. He was shocked by the Arisi attack.

"I would never have thought they would have risked that. I wonder if they really are strong enough now to resist us or whether this was just an opportunistic attack. I will make some further enquiries. I will also make sure that we send an armed vessel to support you when you return to S211-376."

Landro, Vendra and Tzok shared their thoughts about what to do regarding Earth.

Vrin thought hard for a moment before replying. "Do you really think that the humans on Earth can become valued members of the galaxy and not just another group like the Arisi? You may talk of restricting their ability for interstellar travel but we all know that now they know it is possible, they and their increasingly sophisticated computers will solve the physics needed. Then what do we do?"

The debate continued and in the end Vrin agreed to present their ideas to the council.

Despite a fair degree of opposition, the plans outlined by the team were supported by the council.

They prepared to return to Earth but had to wait a further week while repairs were made to *Touching the Heavens*. Finally, it was ready and in no time, they were back in the solar system, cruising past Saturn, Jupiter, Mars and back into Earth's orbit.

The ship remained cloaked as they took up orbit high above the Earth. They all, particularly Tzok, felt that it was safer to be cloaked, not just in case one of the Earth's powers tried something stupid, but also in case the Arisi were prowling around. They had found no trace of them but their ship or ships would also be cloaked, and the Arisi's cloaking technology matched that of the Sirians.

They took a moment to review the events and developments of the two weeks that they had been away.

"Look at this," said Vendra, shocked.

The computer displayed a summary compilation of huge earthquakes and volcanic eruptions in Indonesia and the Philippines, which had triggered deadly tsunamis. The coasts of Indonesia, Thailand, Malaysia, India, Bangladesh and Sri Lanka had been devastated with a loss of life in the millions. Several islands in Micronesia had also been destroyed. The volcanic eruptions were hitting many areas with layers of ash, and air travel across the region had been badly disrupted. As they struggled to take in the scale of the disaster, the computer also brought up headlines, such as 'Where were the Sirians?', with reports asking why they had not intervened as they had on the La Palma earthquake.

"We really are in a race against time," said Landro. He sent a message to Polly telling her that he would be asking the UN to hear him in three days' time. He sent the same message to the other heads of state and to the UN secretary general as well as broadcasting the message to the world's media. Later that evening he rang Polly and gave her a summary 'for her ears only' of his meetings with the council, and what he was proposing to say.

Polly thanked him for sharing the information and gave him an update of what had been happening since he left. She was on her own during the call and she felt a slight concern that every contact with Landro was supposed to be recorded. But at the same time, she trusted Landro (I hope that it is not a mistake, she thought to herself) and felt pleased that he wanted to keep the private link with her. As he concluded what he was proposing to say and after they had discussed it, she asked him how it felt to be back in Qrxa.

"I have travelled a great deal, as you know, but I always see Qrxa through new eyes when I return. That has been particularly true this time. Despite your problems, Earth is one of the planets with the greatest riches I have ever seen – your oceans, your landscapes, your monuments, your music and art. Qrxa is very technologically advanced but it is more monotone than Earth. That is probably why I am now working hard to find solutions to help you rather than insisting that you find all the solutions yourselves." He paused for a moment before adding, "That said, Polly, it would be good if you could see Qrxa sometime…and some of the other worlds in the galaxy. When all of this has played out, I hope we can arrange it."

"I would like that, really like that, Landro," said Polly,

without thinking. She suddenly felt annoyed with herself for sounding like an over-enthusiastic schoolgirl. She hurriedly added, "Of course, it will be very difficult and I must make sure that I don't do anything to compromise what we are trying to achieve here on Earth." She groaned inwardly – that sounded even worse. Let's try just being honest, she thought, and took a deep breath.

"You know, Landro, I find all this really difficult. I really like our conversations but we have met in such extraordinary circumstances that finding the balance between managing my role as the prime minister and principal intermediary between you and the UN on the one hand, and getting to know you as a person on the other, which I would like to do, is really hard. I don't know how we will ever manage it." She felt a wave of relief now that she'd finally said it.

"I agree, Polly. I would like us to have time to get to know each other better. In fact, I would really like that. But we have to find a way forward to get Earth back on track first, and I am aware that even having these calls with you may not actually be helping you. That said, I don't intend to stop them," he said, laughing.

"Good," said Polly. "I am relieved to hear it."

Before they finished their conversation, Polly felt she needed to bring Landro up to date with what had been happening in his absence. He knew about the volcanoes and expressed concern that there were more to come. He thought that Vendra would have ideas on how to remove the ash from the atmosphere. Polly then told him about her efforts to find out what had happened to Steve, the US president.

When Landro had left for Qrxa, Polly had asked Bryony

134

to connect her to the White House. She had hoped to speak to Steve but it was Tom who came on the line. He explained that Steve was still undergoing a detailed and thorough medical examination and for his own safety was being kept in isolation. He warned Polly that she was getting too close to the Sirians and was being too trusting. Did she really have any idea what they might have done to Steve or Yuri? He finished by saying that he did not think Steve would be back on the scene for some time.

Landro was as shocked as Polly had been at the time.

She told him how she had convened her UN group to try to get some clear proposals agreed. She and her team had made some progress, helped, she noted, by some welcome support from the Russians. Clearly, Yuri Andrinov had been heavily influenced by his talks with the Sirians, although she was aware that apart from saying he was back, he had said little to the Russian people about his experience. However, at least he was back in the picture, which was more than could be said for Steve, about whom she had heard nothing more. There was also help from the European Union, where Aurelie Malmaison had brought her influence to bear. However, there was still little help or support from a number of other countries, notably the United States and China.

Landro did not say a great deal more. He was pleased that Andrinov seemed more cooperative and he confirmed that Polly's progress with the UN group had helped in his discussions with the council.

The call ended. It had been a long call, but Polly was glad that Landro was back and that he had phoned her. She had mixed feelings about their more personal exchange – glad to have said it, but concerned that perhaps she was building some false hopes for herself and was just being naïve.

Chapter 26

The next day at the UN, John Redlan, the US ambassador, expressed anger at what he regarded as the peremptory tone of Landro's request. Then to Polly's surprise he said that the acting US president wished to address the assembly in two days' time and asked that all heads of state attend. She tried to contact Tom to find out what this would be about but he could not be reached. The British ambassadors to the UN and the United States did not have any helpful insights either.

Two days later, Tom addressed a crowded assembly. Almost all heads of state were present. Polly found it ironic that the United States could still command such attention, yet the first visitor from another planet failed to attract equal interest.

Tom began his speech. "Mr Chairman, Secretary General, my fellow Heads of Government, Prime Ministers and Ambassadors, you are all aware of the Sirian's peremptory demand to address this assembly tomorrow. I do not propose to resist this demand. I do not know what he will say but I imagine that it will be more threats and warnings about the end of the world, restated requirements for us to make totally unreasonable changes to our lives and to restrict the natural future of humankind to move in due course off this planet and to take our place among the other races of the galaxy. The Sirian media that was streamed to us has shown us the other worlds and other races with whom we should be dealing and trading as equals.

"I believe that that opportunity can still be ours but without the unreasonable and extreme changes that Landro is seeking." Tom paused to take a sip of water. "You have heard references to US contact with other extra-terrestrial races. I do not refer only to Roswell. The US has for some time had contact with another race colloquially known as the Tall Whites but who call themselves the Arisi. For reasons similar to those for keeping Roswell quiet, we have not shared this information. Our relationship with the Arisi has involved us providing a base here on the Earth and on the Moon in return for technology. It was this shared base on the Moon that the Sirians attacked. Subsequently, of course, we all saw the Sirians destroy an Arisi vessel.

"The Arisi have a long history with the Sirians and their council. In their view the Sirians constantly try to control and to restrain. They themselves have fought against the council several times. They have been a good ally to the US. Despite the Sirian attacks, they returned last week and made it clear that they are prepared to be a good ally to Earth just as they have been to the US. They believe that they and humans are natural allies. They are prepared to defend Earth, with force if necessary, from any impositions that the Sirians may seek to make. They are also prepared to help us, in alliance with them, to spread to other planets, other star systems. The Arisi offer no threats, only opportunities. This has to be the way forward for us."

The chamber was filled with lively chatter, and several nations indicated they wished to speak.

President Andrinov rose and spoke first. "Mr Vice President," he said pointedly, "it pains me that I still do not see your president here, and also that I have not been able to speak to him since he and I returned from our enforced sojourn on the Sirian ship. I learnt a great deal during that stay, not least about your Arisi friends. You omitted to mention that the Sirians did not attack the Arisi vessels and facilities on the Moon, only those of the US, facilities about which, I would remind you, the US had chosen not to inform other nations. They of course attacked the ship we were on, knowing full well that your president and I were on board. That does not suggest close allies to me. I also learnt from all that I was shown on the Sirian ship about the wars with the Arisi and others like them, how they exploit weaker races for their own good and benefit. I never thought that I would describe us humans as a weaker race but the fact is that in this galaxy we are like teenagers, even children. I do not believe that the Arisi would have our best interests at heart but only their interests. I do not know what Landro and Vendra will say tomorrow but we must listen to them before we take any rash decisions."

Sweating profusely, he sat down.

Polly was impressed and surprised. Her phone buzzed. Aurelie had sent her a message saying pretty much the same thing.

A string of speakers followed. Some supported the US; others said they needed to wait to see what the following day would bring.

Up on *Touching the Heavens*, Landro, Vendra and Tzok were taken aback by Tom's reference to the Arisi.

"They must have outstanding stealth capabilities. Did you pick up anything when we returned to this system?" he asked the computer.

"I am checking our probes again but nothing came up automatically," replied the computer.

"And where are they now? Presumably at Nellis." Landro paused for a moment. "We need to get a message back to Vrin and Qrxa. Vrin said he would send support but now it may be more urgent than we thought. We also need to make sure that we mask our own movements as much as possible, particularly when using *Sumer* and the little shuttles."

"We can extend the shields on the main ship to protect us," said Vendra and instructed the computer to reset the shields to this effect.

"As for tomorrow, I will need to change my message and address the role of the Arisi head on. I am pleased that Yuri spoke up but it does not help that Steve is still being held and effectively sidelined."

"Perhaps we can do something about that," said Vendra, thoughtful. "We know where he is."

Chapter 27

The following morning, a heavily cloaked *Touching the Heavens* moved very slowly into low-earth orbit. *Sumer*, also cloaked, moved gently away from the main ship and dropped down until it was only a couple of hundred feet above the UN building.

Vendra had been watching carefully for any other perturbations that might indicate an Arisi vessel on the move but found nothing. Landro stepped into the shuttle and moved swiftly down to the UN building entrance. A shimmer around him was the only indication that he had not only his own shields up and working but an additional shield projected from *Sumer*. He entered the building, greeted the chairman and the secretary general and made his way to the podium.

As he looked round the chamber, he suddenly heard gasps as Steve, the US president, entered and headed for the seat currently occupied by the US ambassador. Tom had decided not to attend this meeting, given what had happened to Steve the last time. The US ambassador looked startled. After a brief exchange, he rose and gave Steve his seat. The US president nodded to the Russians and to Landro.

Landro began. "Three weeks ago, I returned to my home world to discuss with the council plans that might help you here on Earth meet the challenges that I laid down to you when I first spoke to you. I am aware that some progress has been made by the group that the UK prime minister has been leading…" Landro looked across to Polly and smiled. "But I am also aware that that group has not had as much support as it needs. There are still countries that do not understand the depth of the issues facing you all and are looking for easy options.

"I recognise that what you heard yesterday from the US acting president about his discussions with the Arisi and their apparent offer to help may have seemed attractive to some. As the Russian president said yesterday, the Arisi and their ways are well known in the galaxy. They do indeed offer to help races that are on the edge of achieving a certain technological level but do so to further their own ends. In certain cases that help has led to the destruction of that race and of their home planet. Nothing they have ever done has helped address the issues you face here, and if you believe that the Arisi will share anything but their most basic technologies with you, you are very much mistaken. They may help you reach other planets, but as their servants. And nothing they will do will help you save this planet.

"That brings me back to what I discussed with the council. You still need to make radical changes yourselves, in particular reducing the Earth's population. To help achieve that, we – and I am authorised on behalf of the council to propose this – will do the following:

"1. Undertake the terraforming of Mars. It may surprise you to know that remnants of underground cities are already on that planet, and the infrastructure that exists is a good springboard to begin returning the planet of habitability. We believe that we can achieve this within three to five years.

"2. We will provide vessels for interplanetary travel and provide the technology to the UN to enable you to build your own ships.

"3. Should you wish to settle other planets or moons or set up artificial space cities above the Earth, in the asteroid belt, or elsewhere we will assist.

"There are also other suitable planets in the galaxy which are either currently uninhabited by sentient races or where the current technologically advanced inhabitants are prepared to welcome humans, and, indeed, where humans may already live. I believe over time, this could result in the transfer of around 2 billion people.

"I am happy to answer any questions you may have."

There was only silence initially as everyone tried to digest the scale of what he had said. Then Steve spoke.

"Commander, you and I have not had the chance to speak since I returned from your ship three weeks ago. I have also not had the chance to speak to the American people since my return. So my words are to them as well as to you and to the other nations here.

"My stay on your ship gave me a different perspective to that which I previously held. Having seen everything you showed me, having listened to you and your Sirian colleagues, and having talked at length to my Russian colleague, President Andrinov…" at this point Steve looked over to the Russian president and smiled, "I realise that our planet is but a tiny part of something so much bigger. The battles that we have fought among ourselves seem so infinitesimally trivial. I genuinely believe now that we can earn our place on the bigger stage you have shown us but

I know that we do genuinely have to earn it. You, Landro, have offered us help. We can do our bit – I recognise that the US has not yet played a meaningful role in the initiatives that the UN committee chaired by Prime Minister Hawkins has been developing. I hereby commit our resources to that."

Looking directly at Landro, Steve continued, "I believe your route is the right one for us – for all of us – and offers us a better chance in time than any of the other routes we have been offered." Steve sat down, to warm applause.

Back in the White House, Tom Peterson and his team watched aghast. They knew that Steve had disappeared twenty-four hours earlier from the hospital where he was being held, and despite the best efforts of the Security Services, no trace of him had been found. Tom was concerned that Steve would try to go to the UN and had therefore arranged – discreetly – for extra security around the building.

"How the hell did the president get in there? Why didn't the ambassador stop him? I need answers fast. And we need to get hold of him now!" yelled Tom.

Back at the UN, Landro had been answering the many questions that people had. He finished by saying that he would leave the chamber so that the representatives could have their own debate. He would return in two days.

As the proceedings broke for a break, there was much more informal mingling than usual at these events. Steve went to speak to Yuri, where they were joined rapidly by Polly and Aurelie. Bryony and Aurelie's Chef de Cabinet followed them and stood nearby as did the US and Russian ambassadors to the UN. They asked him where he had been and how he had managed to reach the debate.

"After London, I was taken to a secure facility

in Washington. Tom believes that I could have been compromised during my time on Landro's ship and wanted me checked out first. Actually, I don't think he wants me back at all. I understood the logic initially but it became clear that any examinations were pretty cursory, and my efforts to speak to him or, indeed, to any of the team were refused. Then yesterday, I suddenly thought I could hear Landro – very odd since he obviously wasn't there – telling me to go out to the small private garden outside my room. The message in my head was insistent. So, I asked the guard who was always outside the room to let me out and suddenly there was a shimmering light and both the guard and I found ourselves lifted up and into one of Landro's small shuttles. The guard pulled his gun and I was shocked to see that he was aiming it at me! He soon dropped it, holding his wrist in agony. Everything was happening so quickly. The shuttle then docked with *Sumer*, where Vendra met me.

"She explained what was happening and said that it was safest for me to stay on *Sumer* until today's meeting. She sent me down here separately just after Landro came down. The beam dropped me in a small yard by a side entrance but inside the perimeter of the building to avoid any problems with any additional guards. We saw the additional security that had been posted around the building. And so here I am."

The US ambassador was worried. "We need to get you somewhere safe, Mr President."

"We do indeed, but I also need to speak to the American people again and to talk to Tom. How are we going to do that?"

Landro, meanwhile, had, after a conversation with the UN secretary general, been heading to the exit when he heard Vendra's voice.

"Change of plan. We have picked up some indications of an Arisi vessel. We think it may be intending to attack the shuttle when you leave. I want you to go to the exit as if you were going to your shuttle but don't enter it. Step back under the portico and the shuttle will take off as if you were in it. We'll watch what happens."

Landro activated his own shields and did as Vendra had instructed. As the shuttle rose to about 100 feet there was a huge crack as a beam of light engulfed the small vessel. Its shields were soon overwhelmed by the energy beam, and the small craft exploded, its debris floating down into the Hudson River.

Landro had moved rapidly back into the chamber where everyone had heard the bang and were rushing towards the exits. A second loud bang rocked the building. This time it seemed the target had been the front of the building, the portico where Landro had just been. Several people who had headed that way were hit by the debris. Landro headed for the group where Steve was and shouted, "The Arisi attacked the shuttle and are now attacking the building. Follow me!"

The group raced to the terrace overlooking the river. A third blast seemed to hit the chamber itself. Looking up, they could see a spacecraft firing the shots. Suddenly another vessel appeared close to it and fired on the first vessel. The first vessel disappeared, as its cloaking mechanism went up but everyone could see how the shield around it was burning red hot as it tried to dissipate the stream of energy aimed at it. Then it disappeared.

"That's the Arisi vessel trying to escape into subspace – a dangerous thing to do when your shields have been hammered like that," said Landro. "I doubt it's the only one so we need to get you out of here."

A beam gathered them up into a small shuttle that suddenly appeared and transported them into *Sumer*, which moved rapidly away and up to the safety of *Touching the Heavens*.

"What the hell is going on? If that wasn't you firing at the Arisi, who was it?" said Steve.

"It's a council fighting ship. President Vrin said he would send vessels. I didn't realise that he had already done so."

From the monitors, it became clear that there was much more activity than they had realised. Several other ships had appeared and were engaging each other. One vessel, an Arisi ship, had started firing at the UN building again, which now was on fire and about to collapse.

"Oh God, that's awful!" cried Polly. "Why are they doing that?"

"All the planet's leaders are in one place. How better to destabilise the planet? I am surprised that the Arisi would risk this but they have always been unpredictable."

They watched as the battle raged on. *Touching the Heavens* had edged away from the battle zone, her shields fully powered and cloaked, but the crew knew that the weaponry they faced could still do them serious damage. The council ships were prevailing but the fight was more evenly balanced than Landro, Vendra or Tzok would have expected. Two Arisi ships had been destroyed when the others broke off, re-cloaked and headed off into subspace. One council vessel was badly damaged and was heading in their direction.

Tzok de-cloaked, hailed them and offered assistance. Their commander came on the screen. To the surprise of the refugees, as they now felt themselves, a tall human figure appeared. He and Landro spoke and the vessel came alongside.

.

"Their medical facility was damaged so we will take their wounded," said Landro. "Preda is Vendra's and my cousin – I didn't realise that he had been sent. Apparently, Vrin sent five ships here, and they all have humans like Vendra and me among their crews."

"What are the Arisi like?" asked Polly.

To her surprise, Steve replied, "We called them the Tall Whites – humanoid although with distinctively different face shapes and eyes rather like the Sirians, and their skin is very pale – hence our name for them."

"Many of the races in the galaxy are humanoid," said Landro. "It is an efficient model although there are several variations – extra eyes or extra limbs. Then there are the races which are more, what you would call, insectoid. That is also an efficient model, and with many different variations. Add to that the one-off sentient species, such as you saw at the council and in the information we have been streaming, and you can see that sentient life takes many complex forms."

"As for the Arisi," he explained, "they operate on the edge of civilised space, looking for opportunities to enrich themselves and to score points off the council. It's because of races like them that the council is so nervous about having other unpredictable races like humans roaming the galaxy. And they certainly don't want two such races acting in collaboration."

The computer told them that a space bridge had been established between the two vessels. Landro and Vendra headed off to help bring aboard the casualties, take them to the medical centre and begin treatment.

Steve, Yuri, Polly and Aurelie, together with their four staff were left in the viewing gallery just above the bridge. The Earth was too far away to see much detail with the naked eye but the viewing panels offered a magnified view. They could see how battered the planet looked. The huge ash clouds over South East Asia were visible, as was the destruction around the coast of India, China and Japan from the earthquakes and tsunamis. As the planet turned they could see the scar where San Francisco had been. There was also the shocking sight of the wreck of the UN building.

"It all looks so fragile from up here," said Polly, a knot in her throat.

"I know," said Steve. "You don't realise it until you are up here looking down on it. I think that was what shook Yuri and me so much."

Yuri grunted in agreement.

Steve continued, "We need to get back down there or at the very least broadcast. People need to know that we are alive. We need to talk to Landro."

Chapter 28

Landro didn't reappear for another hour. Steve, Polly and Aurelie spoke to him about returning but he shook his head.

"It is too dangerous to go back. We don't know whether the Arisi will try again. But I agree that you need to let your governments know that you are back. Perhaps you need to do a joint broadcast. I will set it up."

Half an hour later, the main TV stations had been alerted that there would be a shared broadcast from the leaders of the United States, Russia, the United Kingdom and France. In each country programmes were interrupted with the breaking news. Landro was the first to speak.

"I am speaking to you from a council spaceship some hundreds of miles from the Earth. I have here with me the presidents of the US, Russia and France and the prime minister of the UK whom I was able to rescue from the UN building. They will each speak to you in a moment but first I need to explain to you what happened. You will be aware of the speech by the US acting president to the UN yesterday. He spoke of an offer by the Arisi to help Earth. You saw today what that meant. The Arisi attacked the UN with the intent of killing me and as many of the world's leaders as they could. They wish to destabilise your planet in order to control it themselves, either directly or with the help of certain countries.

"I cannot pretend to you that I know what is going to happen next. I do not know if the Arisi have departed permanently or are planning to return and continue the fight. The council has sent armed vessels to defend the Earth and to prevent the chaos that the Arisi will wish to bring. As soon as possible the leaders who are with me will return to their respective countries."

With that, Steve, Yuri, Polly and Aurelie all spoke, confirming Landro's story. Landro rounded off, promising to provide regular updates as things became clearer.

After the general broadcast, Yuri, Polly, Steve and Aurelie contacted their own staff, advising the senior members of the government and senior staff to move to safe locations for the time being. They made a personal broadcast for their own nations, referring back to the general broadcast, urging people to remain calm while the situation became clearer.

"Not that they will," said Polly. There had already been reports of people rushing to supermarkets to stock up, and in parts of London, Paris and major US cities there were dangerous confrontations between crowds and the police.

"Can you blame them?" said Steve. "Landro's arrival put everyone on edge and just as that was starting to calm down, they suddenly find themselves in the middle of what seems like a science-fiction battle – except in this case it is our planet that is being hit. I wish I knew what Tom was up to. I need to contact him and find out if I can trust him."

Air Force One was in the air, heading away from Washington towards Nellis when Steve got through.

Tom was so angry, he could barely speak. "Can't you see, Steve, that you and the others are being manipulated? That's why I didn't let you back into the White House. You've been taken over. You believe this crap about the Arisi attacking, but what proof is there? It could have all been staged by Landro and his buddies. We know what they can do with their technology, projecting hologrammatic simulations. And it is just as logical for the council to want to take the world's leaders out as it is for the Arisi. After all, it is Landro who has been threatening us, not the Arisi, who so far have been real allies of the US. Try thinking this through, and start thinking about what is best for the US as well."

With that, he rang off and turned to the team around him. "Do we know anything more about the plans of the Arisi?" he barked at the secretary of state. "Are they coming back or have they abandoned us?"

"The envoy says that they had been surprised to find so many council vessels had arrived, so their fleet is regrouping and getting reinforcements. But you can ask the envoy himself when you get to Nellis."

Back on *Touching the Heavens*, Steve was shaken. He turned to Landro. "He could be right. You could be manipulating us all, and this could all be a false-flag event."

They had not noticed that Vendra was back in the room. Her voice surprised them. "Yes, it could and while challenging for me to do so, I could have staged that or something equally convincing. But I didn't. We didn't," she added, looking at Landro and Tzok. "It would make no sense at all for us to destabilise the planet as we address the environmental issues. The world is challenged enough without us adding that to the mix. But for the Arisi it makes total sense, particularly if they are supported by the Americans, which is looking very likely now. Do we know where the acting president is going?" she asked the computer.

"His plane – my plane," interjected Steve angrily, "is heading west, possibly to Nellis or that area. We believe that some Arisi may either still be there or have returned. I need to get back and stop this madness," he shouted.

"We all need to get back," added Polly, and looked at Landro.

"I agree," he said, "but we need to make sure that it is safe. You have let your governments know that you are safe. I suggest you each make contact again and tell them that you will be back as soon as possible."

Yuri and the European leaders made their calls. Steve tried to reach his VP but without success.

Vendra was planning the returns when suddenly the computer spoke.

"I am picking up the turbulence of several vessels emerging near the Earth. I am reducing our own power systems to a minimum to avoid detection. Please avoid all communications."

Startled, nobody said anything, as requested. In the control room the screens showed one, two, three, four... and finally twelve large vessels uncloaking and heading towards Earth. The vessels spread out and, apart from one that headed towards the southern US, the others headed for large conurbations, stopping several hundred feet above them.

Polly and Aurelie held their hands to their mouths in horror as they saw the vessels come to a stop over London and Paris. Yuri grunted when a couple of minutes later, a large vessel halted over Moscow. The whole procedure took no more than thirty minutes. From the larger vessels, smaller ships emerged and took station over other strategic areas.

Polly looked at Landro and caught his eye. "What is happening?" she mouthed.

"Arisi," he mouthed and turned his attention back to the screen.

Tzok motioned to him and Vendra. He had a small pad on which he wrote something.

There was the slightest tremor in the ship and it became clear that it was gently moving further away from Earth. Suddenly the scene on the screens scrambled and only static could be heard.

Vendra turned to the others. "It was unsafe to stay there. Those were Arisi vessels and there were too many of them. Fortunately, our damaged warship made the jump back to Sirius just as the Arisi emerged. That probably helped mask our own presence. We think one council warship has remained in the area but we are not risking communications."

"Vendra, where are we now?" said Polly.

"We are heading to Sirius and our home planet of Qrxa. I am sorry. It was not the plan, but it would have been totally unsafe to try to return you to your countries. We have left a small craft behind with two crew who will try to monitor what is going on and transmit whatever they can back to us."

Landro seemed pensive. "It may actually be an advantage to have you with us. We will talk to Vrin and the council about what to do next and it can only help that he will meet some of Earth's leaders."

Polly stared at him and at Vendra. "What about my sons?" Tears welled up in her eyes.

Aurelie come over and put an arm round her. "I'm sure that your staff will look after them and take them to a safe location. You already said that key people should head out from London. There's nothing more that we can do from here."

"I know. It's just... I feel so helpless." Her voice trailed away for a moment. "And Bryony, I'm sorry. You're in the same position."

Chapter 29

Two days later, the computer announced that the ship would be emerging from subspace. Initially, they had spent several hours during the voyage talking through the options. It was fruitless, they realised, as they had no idea what the Arisi were planning or what the US acting president's role was – indeed, whether he knew what was going on in the first place. On Vendra's recommendation, they had gone to clean up and to rest. Fortunately, the crew numbered far below the ship's passenger capacity so there were enough cabins for everyone. Nobody had a change of clothes but to their amazement, the computer produced avatars for everyone, helping them design what they wanted, and within a couple of hours they had additional clothing. The computer even produced additional jewellery for the four women, much to Polly and Aurelie's amusement and delight.

At the computer's announcement, they reconvened in the main saloon just below the control area. Landro came down from the bridge.

"Welcome to my world," he said. "These are not the circumstances for your visit that we had envisaged but I think it is a special day – the first time in over 20,000 years that inhabitants of Earth have come here." He briefed them on what to expect, reassured them on the gravity, which was similar enough to Earth's, and on the air, also similar enough to Earth.

They all stared at the unfamiliar system as *Touching the Heavens* emerged. Sirius was a binary system, and the first thing that struck them was the two suns.

"How my sons would love to see this," reflected Polly.

The ship worked its way past the outer planets before stopping at one of Qrxa's three moons, which had a docking facility. They headed not for the facility but for *Sumer*, which slipped away from the main ship and headed towards the planet.

Gradually Qrxa edged into full view, drawing gasps from them all. Just as Landro had described, the main planet was connected by a sky elevator to a huge artificial habitat above the surface. There were pods pointing in every direction coming out from the central core. Other habitats could be seen at similar altitudes above the planet's surface, also joined by sky elevators. A closer examination revealed that some looked more industrial, and one, the one towards which they were heading, was clearly the space port that they had all seen so many months earlier in Landro's presentation and in the message from Vrin.

From close up, the eight visitors from Earth were suddenly aware of the structures' huge scale.

Yuri, who had said little since their enforced departure from Earth, turned to Steve. "How puny our world must seem compared to this! Our biggest structures look like children's toys." He paused. "You know, Steve, we need to be a part of the confederation. I cannot believe that whatever the Arisi might offer could rival this."

Steve replied, "Well, the Arisi's technology is clearly far more superior to ours as well. Just look at those ships that arrived. But yes, I agree with you. Although they didn't share a great deal with our people at Nellis, we never had the impression that they had this level of technology. It really is awe-inspiring."

Once they had docked, Landro asked the group to wait while he disembarked and made arrangements. He came back twenty minutes later and led them out into the habitat.

"What do you call this?" asked Polly.

"Space Docking Station Number 2," said Vendra, laughing. "The Sirians named it."

"What is wrong with the name?" asked Tzok. "It is precisely correct. This was the second docking station to be built."

"So how did *Touching the Heavens* get its name?" asked Aurelie.

"That was Landro's name for it. We call it Research Vessel Number 2," said Tzok. "That is a more accurate and appropriate name, in my view."

"Do Sirians tell jokes?" Polly whispered to Landro.

Landro smiled. "Yes, but we do not understand them any more than they understand our humour," he said, adding that he had been struck by how much he had understood most of the humour he had found on Earth.

"Common humanity!" replied Polly.

They disembarked, all feeling that this was a momentous experience. As they came out of the docking tunnel, they entered a large hall. It was full of seats, but of many differing sizes and shapes. Polly thought that made sense given the differing shapes of the people she had seen in the material shown by Landro. She also noticed that she felt quite light and had more spring in her step.

"Gravity here is actually nine tenths of that on Earth – enjoy it! On the ship it was closer to Earth's," said Landro.

A group standing at the back of the hall now approached them. Polly recognised one human as Preda, Landro and Vendra's cousin. He spoke briefly to Landro. Another tall human came forward, accompanied by two children. He went to Vendra, took her hand and they briefly touched heads. Vendra turned to the others and said, "This is my husband, Korodo, and my two children, Koroda and Vendro." There was some confusion as no one could decide the right way to greet each other but it was all light-hearted. The families then stepped aside as two Sirians stepped forward.

"Welcome back. Your news has shocked the council, and Vrin has asked that we go to see him as soon as possible."

Polly was amazed how easily she understood what they were saying – Vendra had given them all implants so that they could hear the statement in their own languages.

Aurelie turned to Vendra. "Is there a chance of a break? I am exhausted. We have hardly slept and I am wary of a long meeting with your chairman when my brain is both tired and brimming over with new experiences."

Steve started to argue that they could all manage when Vendra replied, "There are no formalities on arriving here. We checked you all out on the ship for any diseases or viruses. The meeting with Vrin will be short and it is mainly a courtesy. Then we will take you to our guest quarters and you can rest. Our days are similar to yours. In Earth terms it takes twenty-five hours for a full rotation. However, up here you are in sunlight most of the time. It is very rare for both suns to be out of sight."

They were loaded on to a small buggy with seats adapted to their respective sizes. It took them to the space elevator and as it descended they could see the underneath of the space habitat and just how extensive it was.

"How long did it take you to build that?" asked Steve.

"Less time than you would expect. The original planning was what took time. The plans were then loaded into constructor robots and off they went. They worked all the time and many of the pieces are actually spun metal."

At the base of the elevator, they were whisked through the crowds of people waiting to board and taken to another shuttle, which ascended to an aerial trackway and at a speed that seemed dangerously fast, swept them through and mainly over a city below. They suddenly came to an area of vegetation, which Landro explained was the park where the council had its offices and meeting chambers. The shuttle swept on and into a station.

They alighted. Two Sirians escorted the party on foot through several corridors until they reached two large doors. One of the escorts pressed a button on the door and after a brief moment, the doors swung back to reveal a large room, with the adaptable chairs as Polly now recognised them to be and a large picture window looking out over the park. She was startled by the different nature of the vegetation, much of which seemed to be blue-ish rather than the green she had expected. Illogical to assume that, she thought.

In the middle of the room stood Vrin, two other Sirians and another human. The human had similar features to Landro but was taller and had darker hair. Vrin stepped forward and introduced himself to each of them with a small wave of the hand, just as Tzok had greeted them.

"Welcome to Qrxa," he said. "I am sorry that you are here in such difficult times." He introduced the two Sirians as Truk, his military adviser and Vryk, his deputy military adviser. He introduced the human adviser as Porten, responsible for primitive worlds.

That puts us in our place, thought Polly, but compared with this world we clearly are pretty primitive. From the looks on her colleagues' faces, it was clear that they were thinking the same thing.

Landro spoke. "We are glad to be back. I did have concerns that we might have problems leaving S211-376." In an aside to his companions from Earth he clarified, "Your solar system." Turning back to Vrin he asked, "Have you had any further information from the probes or the military vessel you left behind?"

Vrin replied, "I am conscious that you will be tired, and I do not want to keep you too long. But yes, we have received messages. The warship has retired to nearer P4, the planet you call Mars. The small probe, however, has been able to get closer to Earth and to avoid detection. It appears that the twelve Arisi ships have remained over the cities where they initially settled. You may not have seen that they sent out smaller vessels over other key locations. There has been no fighting, although it does appear that certain military facilities in Russia have been destroyed and an attempted retaliation failed. This is your country, President Andrinov, I believe." He turned briefly to Yuri, who paled. "We have also picked up this broadcast from the president of the United States."

"Vice president!" said Steve, angrily.

Vrin paused a moment, slightly uncomfortable. "President, actually. He has been sworn in."

A screen emerged from above a table and a voice announced, "The President of the United States of America."

Tom appeared. "My fellow Americans, good evening. This is the first time that I address you formally as your president. Removing Stephen McIerney, our previous president, was not a decision taken lightly but following his first, and now second, abduction by the alien Landro, we believed his judgement had been compromised. He no longer had the best interests of this nation at heart. Moreover, we don't know where he currently is. In these circumstances Cabinet has decided that it is in the best interests of the nation to declare Steven McIerney unfit to continue as president. This nation needs and deserves strong and effective leadership at this time and consequently Congress has confirmed that I should now assume the presidency.

"These are deeply challenging times and I will do my utmost to ensure that our interests are protected against the threats that Landro and his so-called council have made against us. We saw their true colours in the destruction of the United Nations building with the deaths of so many of our world leaders, a destruction that Landro tried to blame on the Arisi, and we were only protected from further destruction by the welcome arrival of ships from the Arisi. As you know from my speech to the UN the day before the attack, we in the US have had regular contact with the Arisi for some decades and we have no doubt that they have both the interests of the United States and of humanity as a whole at heart. The arrival of their ships has led to the departure of the Sirians, and by placing these ships across the planet in strategic locations we believe that the council will not return.

"We are fortunate to have established a good relationship with the Arisi, and I personally met their ambassador yesterday at Nellis. It makes sense for the United States to keep the lead in this relationship as we discuss the opportunities that will now open up for us to go out beyond this planet and to take our rightful place among spacefaring nations. I will consult with our allies as and when it is appropriate but in the current challenging times, the United States will, as it has in the past, take on the mantle of protecting the best interests of everyone on this planet.

"Finally, I would say that it is important that we as a planet speak with one voice when communicating with the Arisi, and I therefore look forward to the support not just of the American people but of all the people of this planet as we develop our future.

"God Bless America, and God bless everyone on Earth."

Steve was appalled, as was Landro. Vrin raised his hand and said, "We will not debate this now but it is clear that we are dealing with a coup engineered by the Arisi in which your country, or at least your colleague," he looked at Steve, "is being used as a puppet. Talk among yourselves and we will meet at the same time tomorrow. Landro and Vendra, please remain with me. Porten will take the rest of you to your accommodation. Landro will join you later." With that, Vrin gave a small wave and turned to Landro.

Polly and the others felt it was a rather abrupt dismissal but Polly remembered Landro's comments about the Sirians being very transactional. Landro clearly recognised their reaction. Turning and smiling, he said, "I look forward to seeing you all later."

They were led out of the main building and into a small shuttle. Less than five minutes later they stepped out into what appeared to be the other side of the park.

Porten had said very little but as they disembarked he

rather unexpectedly said, "I am delighted to meet you all. To meet humans from a planet where I have had no contact is very special, and I look forward to getting to know you better."

He handed them a screen and asked each of them to look at it while their profiles were memorised.

"Your rooms are this way," he said and led them through a corridor to the right to a series of guest rooms. Each room had been illuminated with the flag of their country. Polly's and Bryony's rooms were opposite each other, and everyone else's rooms were nearby but along another corridor.

Polly had not been sure what to expect but the room was unexpectedly normal – a bed, sofa, chairs, a desk with a screen on it and a bathroom in which everything was familiar. The only surprise was when the computer spoke to her in Vendra's voice.

"Hello Polly, I hope you find everything to your liking. The new clothes that were made for you on Research Vessel Number 2 are in your closet together with some additional clothes and shoes which I hope you like. If you wish to talk to your colleagues just ask the computer to connect you, or of course knock on their doors. However, please don't leave the complex until we have had a chance to show you around. Can I suggest you take the chance to rest and to try to sleep and we will aim to meet up in ten Earth hours' time. Your clocks have been set for Earth hours."

Polly did not need to be asked twice. Despite everything that was going around in her head, she was exhausted and had no trouble falling asleep.

Chapter 30

Polly was awoken by the gentle ringing of an alarm and a voice, not Vendra's this time, gently asking her to wake up.

When she emerged from the bathroom, and dressed, the computer suggested that she join her colleagues in the lounge at the entrance to the complex.

"Please follow the lights that will appear as you leave your room."

Polly obeyed and found all her colleagues apart from Aurelie already gathered. Aurelie joined them shortly afterwards. Everyone felt refreshed and surprised at how well they had slept. There was a range of food on a table and everyone found something to their liking. They had just finished eating when Landro arrived.

After asking how they had slept, he made the chairs arrange themselves into a circle, and the group sat down.

"I am conscious that you must have felt that Vrin was a bit abrupt yesterday. He genuinely welcomes you but as you are finding out, Sirians do not see any need to observe what you would call niceties.

"We had a long conversation after you left, with Porten rejoining us. Vrin wanted to understand what had been happening and to get the views of Vendra, Tzok and myself. He is talking today to his other advisers and then tomorrow to the council. He says he will therefore not see you today but tomorrow.

"I know you will be disappointed but the upside is that I can show you a little of Qrxa, or at least of our main city here."

"What is the capital called?" asked Steve.

"The Sirian name translates as Number 1 City," said Landro, laughing. "And before you ask, there are indeed Numbers 2, 3, 4 et cetera cities.

"You have seen a lot from the information we streamed on Earth about our planet, but perhaps a visit to the market will be of interest. And just to warn you, you will see many other sentient species there. Unlike on Earth, feel free to stare. Everyone will stare at you as well. News of what has been happening on Earth has been in the news here, and news of your arrival was broadcast yesterday. Even for here, you are celebrities!"

A small shuttle took them into the built-up areas. They were all struck by the soaring towers with aerial skyways dominating the landscape. Occasionally there was a larger formal building. There were a lot of parks where they could see people walking and playing. As well as Sirians and humans, there were several other species – some taller than the humans, some with additional limbs but nearly all humanoid. Occasionally there was an insect-looking creature with what Landro explained were breathing apparatus around their heads.

"The atmosphere on Qrxa generally only suits humanoid species but other visitors want to come here as tourists, and so they adapt. We create off-world habitats for those who want to live and work here, with atmospheres suited to their own origins. The market we are going to is unusual. Most food, clothing et cetera is produced by replicators but some people specialise in the old ways of production. Ironically the imperfections in a handmade hanging or floor covering make it more valuable than the perfect goods produced by the replicators."

"Is there food in the market – meat, fruit?" asked Aurelie.

"No. Sirians have never eaten meat from other species, and generally speaking most other humanoid species, including humans here, have also stopped doing so. That said, the replicators produce food that tastes like meat, as you found out on the ship. However, there is produce that grows on the land and in the oceans here. None of it will be recognisable and some of it will taste odd on your palates. You will see that each stall, as you would call them, has a screen displaying suitable and unsuitable food for the different species."

Polly and the others found it fascinating as they went round the market, as much for the mix of species there as for the products themselves.

Feeling rather like a tourist, she asked Landro how she would buy anything if she wanted to.

"Yes, you can buy things or rather I will buy them for you. Vrin has given me an allowance to cover all your needs." He produced a small handheld device with which he paid for the mixture of, to them, exotic goods that they each bought.

They returned to the shuttle, which took them up to a nearby hilltop from where they could look out over the seemingly endless vista of towers, aerial roadways and green parks. They could also see the sky elevators stretching way up into the sky and the sun glittering on the undersides of the off-world habitats. Several moons could be seen, some quite faint, as well as the two suns.

They returned via one of the parks they had previously walked through and examined the different plant life. Large insects were everywhere but there was nothing resembling a bird.

Once they had returned to the guesthouse, Landro said, "You may wish to use the exercise and recreation area. Some of the equipment will be familiar to you from your gyms on Earth but other areas such as the zero-gravity float room will be different. You should find suitable clothing in your rooms."

Everyone, including Yuri, wanted to try what was on offer, and they all emerged, rather self-consciously, in what had been provided for them – skin-tight costumes similar to those worn by Landro and Vendra.

"I am glad my children cannot see me now!" said Yuri.

"For the first time ever, I wish I had gone to the gym," said Aurelie.

Polly, who did work out, rather liked the costume and she blushed slightly when she saw Landro looking at her with what she hoped was approval.

"You see, Polly," said Aurelie, "I told you men are totally predictable."

Polly blushed even more.

The zero-gravity room was a wonderful place to float around in. Yuri looked the happiest they'd ever seen him.

"How do I get one of these back on Earth?" he asked Landro. "I feel thirty years younger."

The mention of Earth made them all reflect as had the mention of children earlier, and the mood became more serious. They left the room, changed back into their regular clothes and met up with Landro, and Vendra who had joined them. Over a meal they discussed the options.

"We all want to go back to Earth," said Steve, "and be with our families. We really appreciate how you have helped us but we feel useless here."

"You are not at all useless here, and I think your presence is important in the discussions of the council," said Vendra. "Of course, you must go home but surely it needs to be when it's safe enough…"

No further news had been received from Earth and no one had any ideas on how to stop the Arisi or the aggressive line that the United States was taking. Despondent, they all headed off to their rooms. Landro accompanied Polly and Bryony to their corridor. After Bryony had wished them goodnight, Landro and Polly chatted further.

"Why don't you come in?" said Polly, slightly surprising herself. She realised how reassuring she found Landro's presence, as she processed everything that was going on and reflected how her whole world had changed since his arrival. Landro finally stood up and said he probably needed to head back to his own room. Polly paused a moment and then, again rather to her surprise, said, "Would you like to stay?"

When Polly awoke the next morning, Landro had gone. Her communication device beeped and a small heart appeared. She showered and went to join the others.

Aurelie smiled at her as she sat down. "You are glowing, Polly. You clearly slept well!"

Polly blushed and replied, "I feel good, Aurelie, and thank you, I slept as well as I have in a very long time!"

No more was said, but Bryony, who had also noticed

how bright her boss seemed, felt that given all the strain her boss had been under, it could only be for the best.

Landro and Vendra arrived shortly afterwards. Vendra smiled at Polly, heard her animated chatter and then looked briefly at her brother, who studiously ignored her. She laughed to herself.

Landro spoke. "Vrin has completed his discussions and would like to see everyone. We'll leave in an hour."

They chatted among themselves until Landro returned to advise them that the shuttle was ready.

The group entered Vrin's large office where he was again accompanied by various advisers.

After initial greetings, Vrin began. "The view of the council is that we cannot allow the Arisi to take control of your planet and solar system. We have two choices: one military and the other diplomatic. We can attack the Arisi ships that are on Earth, and we believe that we can destroy them. There will inevitably be huge casualties among the human population because of the proximity of the Arisi vessels to major centres of population. Indeed, we assume that the Arisi placed their vessels where they did, not just to intimidate the Earth's population but because they believe we would not attack them. This might not be a bad outcome from the point of view of the council as it would achieve one major aim, which is to reduce the number of humans on the Earth."

Steve and everyone in the group looked aghast and were about to voice their concerns when Vrin said, "There is the second option: diplomacy. But first I must ask you humans from S211-376 a question. If we can recover your planet from the Arisi, do you believe that you can persuade your people to accept the proposals that Landro made at your United Nations just before the attack?"

Steve answered first. "I am confident that we can. My own views, like those of President Andrinov, have changed completely since the arrival of *Touching the Heavens*."

Vrin frowned until Landro interjected, "Chairman, that is what we call Research Vessel 2."

Vrin's frown deepened. "Please continue," he said.

"All of us have now seen at first hand a future that we would want the Earth to be part of. I cannot give any guarantee but the four of us make up four of the five members of the UN Security Council and that will carry weight. Of course, following the attack on the UN building we will have many new colleagues whom we will have to get to know but given the aggressive stance of the Arisi, and I am afraid, of the United States, I believe that they will follow us."

He looked at the others for their contributions.

"I agree with President McIerney," said Yuri, "and given the close relationship that we enjoy with China, the fifth permanent member, I believe they will join us."

Polly and Aurelie added their agreement.

Vrin responded, "We now know where the Arisi have their home planet. Preda showed great foresight during the battle and managed to attach a tracker on one of the Arisi ships just before they entered subspace. By good fortune, the ships emerged in a star system where we had recently sent an unmanned probe and it picked up the tracking signal. We have subsequently discreetly checked it out. The world the Arisi have chosen is rather inhospitable but could be made more suitable for them. So the diplomatic solution we would propose would be as follows: we will offer assistance to the Arisi to create a suitable world to live in; we will offer them a deal that brings them within the council's broad oversight but leaves considerable freedom, and in return we will require them to remove their ships from Earth. We will make clear that the council will not allow them to remain on Earth and so they must choose which route to take. Landro tells me that in the language you call English you use the phrase 'an iron fist in a velvet glove'. We have also learnt that there are certain minerals on the Earth that the Arisi want and need to help create a more hospitable atmosphere on their home planet. We can provide them with those minerals as part of the deal."

There was a moment's silence, then Steve spoke up. "I think I speak on behalf of all my colleagues when I say we, of course, support the diplomatic approach first. I just about understand your strategic thinking with the military option but the destruction of Earth's great cities and the huge loss of population would cause chaos on our planet, and not just to humans. So please pursue the diplomatic approach. If you are successful, we will do our utmost to get our fellow leaders to work together and with you to create a sustainable planet and a sustainable future for our people."

He looked at the others who nodded in agreement.

Vrin paused, deep in thought and asked them to leave the room for a few minutes while he talked to Landro and the other advisers.

After a few minutes, the group were asked to return.

"We will follow the diplomatic approach. Our fleet has already been made ready and we will send it immediately to the Arisi planet so that they know that we are serious. We know that most of their fleet was sent to Earth so they will understand that they need to take our offer seriously.

We should have some news within no more than ten Earth days. Until then I suggest you remain here and enjoy our hospitality."

Chapter 31

On Earth, Tom had returned from Nellis Air Force Base where he had spent a few days talking to the Arisi ambassador. He was in the White House as he felt it important to give a sense of normality, even if in reality nothing was normal. He was puzzled that after their initial broadcasts and his call with Steve they had heard nothing more from Landro or from Steve and the others who were with him. The Arisi either didn't have any idea or didn't want to tell him what the council were up to.

After his speech, he had met other leaders at the UN. To his irritation, there was a lot of anger about the US stance and about the presence of the Arisi vessels. The Russian vice president accused the United States of being puppets in the face of what was clearly an occupation – he referred to the destruction by the Arisi of their own military facilities.

"Well, you attacked them!" barked Tom. "What did you expect would happen?" He attempted once more to explain the opportunities offered by the Arisi.

In the meantime, the geological turbulence on the planet continued. There had been further volcanic eruptions, including one near Hawaii which had sent a huge tsunami crashing on to the already battered west coast of the US. The media made the point that this time the Arisi vessels had done nothing to prevent the damage or to help with the casualties.

A week later, the head of Space Command rang Tom to inform him that the Arisi ambassador wanted to meet with him urgently. Tom felt that the ambassador could have come to him but nevertheless boarded Air Force One and headed west.

The ambassador was clearly uncomfortable (to the extent that Tom couldn't deduce anything from the inscrutable features of the Arisi opposite him). A translation device on the table between them translated the harsh guttural language of the ambassador into English.

"Due to unforeseen developments, I regret to advise you that we will be withdrawing our vessels at the end of the week and returning this planet to the oversight of the council. We are prepared to take with us a number of humans. Humans who wish to leave should present themselves a week today below the craft that we have stationed above your cities and military facilities. We will then select those whom we feel can best adapt to a new life. You may care to do so yourself, and you and your family would be welcome. Let me know what you decide."

The ambassador refused to say what had caused the change and brought the discussion to a rather peremptory close.

Tom was shocked. He really thought that the Arisi were the answer to Earth's ambitions. On the way back to Washington, he reflected on the implications of this radical change and it struck him that his own future would be very bleak once Steve returned. Although it was unlikely that Steve would be able to reassume the presidency, he would still, with the support of Landro, be in a very influential, and potentially vengeful, position.

That night, with a heavy heart, Tom spoke to the nation and to the planet, telling them that the Arisi had decided to withdraw but that they would take with them a certain number of humans who wished to leave. He recommended that they do so, reminding them that their future under the council was uncertain. He added, "I intend to leave with the Arisi and look for new opportunities for myself and for my fellow humans who will be coming with me."

A week later, large crowds gathered at the various sites and the Arisi landed their huge ships. Several million had decided to take the risk and had presented themselves, although for most people the suddenness of the decision and the uncertainty about what was on offer meant that they decided to stay and take their chances with the council. The Arisi lined everyone up and scanned as many people as they could with handheld scanners. They seemed to be selecting those who were physically the fittest and healthiest, and couples.

The Arisi vessels lifted off. Those who had not been selected watched the vessels rise until they were specks in the sky and then disappeared completely.

The world waited with bated breath. In America, the new vice president, Morten Cruz, previously the Speaker of the House, who had been sworn in when Tom assumed the presidency, now became acting president. Nobody knew what to expect. Was the world on its own again or would Landro and the four leaders who had gone with him reappear?

Chapter 32

On Qrxa, the group had spent a frustrating and anxious few days. Landro and Vendra had tried to entertain them. Vendra had invited everyone to her off-world home and they had enjoyed going back up the sky elevator and meeting her children and her husband. Landro and Polly had spent a lot of time together, something that even the men in the group began to notice.

Finally they were summoned by Vrin. He told them that the Arisi had accepted the offer and that they should now return to Earth in anticipation. They were delighted.

They returned to the offshore habitat and took *Sumer* up to another research vessel, RV1.

"What is your name for this vessel?" Polly asked Landro.

"I haven't named it yet. What do you think we should call it?"

"I suggest *Redemption*," said Polly. "We have been given a second chance to get things right."

"That's a good name, Polly," said Landro, looking at the others, who nodded in agreement. "*Redemption* it is."

In their desperation to return to Earth, the two days' journey felt like twenty. As they emerged from hyperspace and cloaked themselves, they could see the Arisi vessels moving away from the Earth and into hyperspace. They also picked up Tom Peterson's broadcast.

Vendra interrupted their discussions. "Landro has sent a message to each of your countries and advised them of your return. We will drop each person at their respective capitals. There is a lot to be done. It is clear that there have been riots in many cities as the fear and uncertainty takes hold. Those who could not board an Arisi vessel are feeling particularly angry. We also suggest that you and Landro address the United Nations in three days' time. That will give you all a chance to get up to speed before the meeting."

Redemption stopped in inner-earth orbit. It was still cloaked. Tzok and his team could not find any trace of any remaining Arisi presence but they were taking no chances. They had advised the council warship that had originally been left behind of their presence and they knew that it was also keeping an eye out.

The eight passengers transferred to *Sumer.* From there they moved into smaller shuttles which delivered each of them to the welcoming party in their own country.

Yuri landed in Red Square to cheers from the crowds. He waved and was then taken off into the Kremlin.

Aurelie was similarly welcomed as her shuttle landed outside the parliament in Paris.

Polly and Bryony landed in Hyde Park. Polly thought about just how much had happened since Landro's first, totally unexpected appearance. Their world and their knowledge of the universe and of their own galaxy had changed beyond anything that she might have imagined. As she stepped out of the shuttle, her two sons ran up to her, followed closely by Bryony's two children. Polly hugged her boys and felt the tears rolling down her face. Composing herself, she approached the microphone that had been set up.

"As you can see, I am very glad to be back." She brushed away a tear and put an arm around each boy. "We are living through an extraordinary time. All of us feel that we have been swept up in a science-fiction novel. The reality is that the galaxy and the universe are more like science fiction than we ever realised. We can now be a constructive part of that universe, and my fellow leaders and I are determined that we should be. We are confident that the options given to us by Landro and the council are our best choice, and that living on the margins of that civilisation under the tutelage of the Arisi would have been a very poor choice. We are meeting in three days' time at the United Nations to spell out and discuss our way forward. In the meantime, please stay calm. There is no need to be afraid."

Polly allowed time for questions, and her answers included her explanation of what she believed had happened with the Arisi, together with her own impressions of Qrxa and the Sirians. She then headed to 10 Downing Street.

The shuttle carrying Steve landed outside Congress, at Steve's request. He had decided to land there and not at the White House because whatever his personal views about the way the law had operated, he realised that legally he was no longer president of the United States.

He stepped out of the shuttle. There was a large crowd but they were much more muted than in London or Paris. There were some cheers and some boos. President Cruz came forward and shook his hand warmly.

"Welcome back, Steve. These are strange times. However, I think we can treat you better than on your previous return.

If you are prepared, both Houses of Congress wish to hear from you."

Steve thanked him, congratulated him on becoming president and said he wished to speak to the people gathered on the steps of Congress first. He spoke on similar lines to Polly and as he began to deal with questions from the media he could feel the mood of the crowd warming. When he had finished there were loud whoops and cheers. He walked into Congress.

Three days later, they all gathered in the ballroom of the hotel currently being used by the UN following the destruction of the UN headquarters. Polly couldn't help noticing how many new faces there were as she thought how lucky they had been to escape with Landro from that destruction. She was just thinking about Landro when he entered the room, flanked by Vendra and Tzok. They took their seats in the visiting-speakers' box. The chairman of the assembly, Eduardo Soares, president of Portugal, who had survived the attack, invited Polly to speak first.

Thanking the president, she began. "These have been extraordinary times. Things have changed in a way none of us could have imagined before the arrival of Landro, Vendra and their colleagues from Qrxa. Normally, as prime minister of the United Kingdom of Great Britain and Northern Ireland, I would focus on what was most important for my own country. I still care deeply for my country and what is best for it, but what the last few months, and in particular the last few weeks, have taught me is that in the context of a galaxy that is teeming with other species and civilisations, many far more advanced than ours, our national rivalries are totally insignificant. We need to work together as one planet, to solve the challenges that Landro laid before us so many months ago, and to earn the right to take our place in the community of planets that make up the council. That does not mean we cease to be British, American, Russian, Indian or Chinese, or whatever nationality we are, but in this new universe that we find ourselves in, we have to genuinely think and behave globally. It is no longer enough just to pay lip service to that idea. Our survival and our opportunities as humans depend on it."

She looked over to Landro, and went on. "Thanks to our visitors from Sirius, we now understand our responsibilities as custodians of our planet, our beautiful planet. We need to accept our duty to protect and promote the welfare of the Earth and of all its species. We need to show the planet that she can trust us. This will involve a radically different way of life and of living but it is the only way for us. The Sirians have shown us the way forward. We must follow it, for the sake of humankind here on Earth now and for all future generations."

The events of recent days had had a profound impact on everyone's thinking, and Polly's speech was warmly applauded.

Yuri and Aurelie spoke on similar lines, each adding something about their personal experience on Qrxa.

Then Morten Cruz, who had Steve standing beside him, spoke. "These recent months have been challenging for all the nations of this planet, but they have been particularly challenging for us here, in the United States. Our previous president, Steve McIerney, who is standing next to me and whose term as president, was, I think I can say, unfairly although legally brought to an end, has performed a great service to our nation. His speech to Congress three days ago, where he described what he had seen and learnt on his travels with Landro, have persuaded us that the course described by the United Kingdom is indeed the way we now need to go. The United States will therefore support whatever it takes to solve the challenges that Landro placed before us, and to take our place, as a planet, not as individual nations, in the greater community of planets that we now know is out there."

This received great applause. Other nations spoke, nearly all on the same theme. Crucially China supported the approach, and in the end only a couple of the more theocratic states expressed any reservations.

Finally, the president invited Landro to speak.

"As Prime Minister Hawkins said, these have been extraordinary times, and things have changed in ways none of us, including for those of us from Qrxa, could have imagined. For Vendra and me, it has been an extraordinary experience to connect with humans on the planet from which our ancestors originally came some 20,000 years ago. We have experienced such a sense of common humanity, and it has changed our view on how we need to help you change. More importantly, the recognition of some of your key leaders that you need a different approach to your relationship with this planet, played a key role in persuading the council on Qrxa to take the diplomatic approach in solving the Arisi problem. It was not intentional that I would find myself taking the leaders of the United States, Russia, the United Kingdom and France to Qrxa but there was no doubt that their presence influenced the council in a way I might not have been able to do. You owe them your gratitude.

"There are challenges ahead, and you will all need to agree to endorse the proposals I laid out at my last appearance here. But for the first time, I am confident that with our help, you will solve the challenges facing this planet, and that you will be able to take your rightful place, in time, in the council of the galaxy."

Epilogue

The plan that Landro had spelt out before the UN was the one that was implemented. Over 2 billion people in time relocated to other worlds. Mars was being terraformed and the first colonies were established there within four years. Off-world habitats, connected by sky elevators were constructed and within five years several million people had moved into these. Colonies were established in the asteroid belt. The council had been more generous with sharing their technology than originally suggested. On Earth much of Central Africa, the Amazon basin and extensive parts of Russia had been returned to nature. With a smaller population, there were ambitious plans to return more areas. The number of earthquakes and volcanic eruptions plummeted. If climate change had not been stopped, the planet was at least stabilising. The nation states remained but the UN now had the lead role in the relations with the council. The UN had an elected president: Steve McIerney.

Polly resigned as prime minister a year after they returned and as an MP shortly afterwards. Vrin had proposed that she might work on council diplomacy. She initially thought that he was just accommodating her and Landro's wish to be together but Vrin made it clear that he valued her for her own skills.

"I will never fully understand humans," he said, "but you are clearly a leader who has the focus, logic and drive that I and other Sirians admire, together with what Vendra describes as the Emotional Intelligence so valued by humans and other species. I recognise that Emotional Intelligence is not a trait that we Sirians possess, and that is why we use people like Landro for our diplomacy. I think your skills will be a great asset to the council...if you are prepared to join us. You can of course bring your sons with you. You will be based on Qrxa but will travel widely, mainly with Landro and Vendra, but not always. And we will make sure that you can return regularly to Earth."

Polly talked to her sons and they were thrilled at the idea. Five years later, Polly and Landro had a three-year-old son who, for them, became the symbol of Earth's humans reconnecting with the other humans who had left Earth so many millennia before.

Lightning Source UK Ltd.
Milton Keynes UK
UKHW011244300921
391375UK00003B/58